FREEDOM'S RING

GEMINI JONES, FREEDOM'S RING

By Anya Sharma

Distributed by Smokeshow Publishing

CHAPTER 1:
GEMINI JONES

The lecture hall doors hissed open, a sound like a tired mechanical sigh releasing compressed air – and us. Two hundred students blinking in the sudden assault of the midday GLAMA sun, spilling out not into freedom, but into the milling, branded chaos of the main campus quad. GLAMA – the Greater Los Angeles Metropolitan Area, a sprawling beast that sometimes felt like it was swallowing itself whole – was less a space for learning and more a stage set for the university's image, relentless and unforgiving.

The sun glared off pristine concrete pathways – swept clean every morning by an underpaid, near-invisible crew – and bounced off the aggressively cheerful banners flapping from every strategically placed lamppost. "Unity Through Excellence!" this semester's slogan proclaimed in bold, Sterling Corp-approved sans-serif font. The colors – a vaguely patriotic red, white, and blue, but muted, corporate – felt intentional, designed to soothe and distract.

Last semester it was "Building Tomorrow, Together!" Before that, "Innovation Nation!" The words changed like fashion trends, meaningless syllables focus-grouped into existence, but the underlying message, funded by the university's biggest billionaire benefactor, remained the same: Shut up, smile, consume, and don't question the tuition hikes. Or the new biometric scanners at the library entrance, the ones that replaced the bored security guard who used to just wave you through with a nod.

Last year, you just flashed your ID. Progress, they called it. I saw a news ticker on one of the campus screens this morning – Sterling

Tech "donating" new "community monitoring systems" to underserved neighborhoods. Generous.

A tide of expensive sneakers – gleaming white, limited edition, probably costing more than my entire grocery budget for the month – squeaked on the immaculate concrete. Logo-emblazoned hoodies representing fraternities and sororities, names like Sigma Alpha Money and Delta Delta Delusion, moved in loud, confident packs. Their chatter, a high-pitched, energetic buzz echoing slightly in the wide-open space, seemed composed entirely of weekend plans involving yachts or parental vacation homes, upcoming formals requiring thousand-dollar dresses, and intense debates about which photo filter best conveyed "authentic carefree living." The sound grated, a frequency of privilege I couldn't tune out. These were people who'd never worried about a late fee on a utility bill, let alone the crushing, compound interest accumulating on the mountain of federal and private loans that constituted my "opportunity" here.

Up ahead, near the ironically named "Fountain of Wisdom" (currently spewing recycled, chlorinated water onto imported Italian marble in a display of conspicuous water consumption that felt obscene in drought-prone GLAMA), Chad Broleton the Third held court.

He leaned against a faux-travertine bench with practiced nonchalance, one expensive sneaker crossed over the other, pontificating to Tiffany McSparklepants and her identically highlighted, athleisure-clad sorority sisters about the new city-wide curfew imposed after last night's "disturbances." I saw Rhys trying to edge into their circle, looking awkward, like he wasn't sure what to do with his hands. He offered a comment about the curfew being "a necessary step for public order, right? Like SNN said?"

Chad gave him a blank look before turning back to Tiffany. Rhys flushed, fiddling with the strap of his guitar case, his attempt to mimic Chad's casual lean just making him look out of place. He probably hadn't even registered the increased CPB liaison officer presence on campus lately, or the way certain anti-Sterling street art near the student union kept disappearing overnight, replaced by bland municipal murals.

"...totally sucks," Chad drawled, pausing to run a hand through sandy blond hair that probably required multiple expensive products and a personal stylist to look so effortlessly windswept. "Means pre-gaming has to start way earlier if we want to hit the Westside clubs before ten. Logistics nightmare." He sighed dramatically. "But Dad says it's just temporary, y'know? For *safety*." He delivered the word with an air of profound insight, as if uttering a sacred truth handed down from on high (or, more likely, from his father's corporate security consultant). Tiffany and the clones nodded seriously, their perfectly glossed lips pursed in sympathetic agreement, their eyes reflecting only the blue sky and their own reflections.

Safety. *Whose* safety? Not the kids getting roughed up by GLAMA PD for protesting evictions, that was for sure. The word felt thin, brittle, like cheap plastic stretched too tight over something rotten and crawling. Like the sleek, new biometric scanners flanking the entrance to the student union and the main library, installed silently and without consultation over the summer break. Last year, you just flashed your student ID. A quick wave, a bored nod from the security guard who probably made minimum wage. Now it was press your thumb against the cool, slightly greasy glass plate, wait for the internal whirring, hope the system recognized your unique, digitally captured essence today. Hope the network wasn't down. Hope your print hadn't been smudged by graphite or guitar string grime or the cheap hand lotion you used because the GLAMA air sucked all the moisture out of everything. *Beep. Green light.*

A moment of relief quickly followed by resentment. Progress. Sterling Tech™ logos, small but unmissable like a corporate tattoo, were etched into the brushed metal casings. Of course they were. Sterling's companies seemed to have a lock on every security, surveillance, and data management contract in GLAMA these days. From the cameras on the streetlights – more of them every week, it seemed – to the software running the traffic grid to the damn scanners verifying my right to borrow a library book. Convenient. For him.

GLAMA University. Prestigious. Exclusive. Crawling with the ambitious offspring of the city's elite. Built, according to persistent campus legend and a few hushed mentions in obscure local histories, directly on top of an ancient Tongva burial ground. Sometimes, feeling the weird, hollow energy humming beneath the relentlessly manicured lawns and imported decorative shrubs, I almost believed it. Felt fitting, somehow. Paving over the past, building monuments to wealth on stolen land. The GLAMA way.

I kept my head down, sketchbook clutched like a shield against my chest, my knuckles white. It wasn't just paper and ink; it was armor, a filter, a place to process the relentless psychic static. Hallway and quad navigation was a survival skill here, less about avoiding physical collisions – though the sheer lack of spatial awareness in some of these people was astounding – and more about avoiding the *other* kind of impact: the assumptions, the microaggressions disguised as compliments ("You speak so articulately!"), the judgments veiled in helpful advice ("Have you considered joining the Black Student Union? It's important to find your people!"). It meant avoiding eye contact with anyone radiating that particular brand of manufactured enthusiasm, anyone who might try to recruit me for their acapella group singing sanitized pop covers, anyone asking if I'd "found my community" yet (translation: joined the right clubs, networked with the right future CEOs, assimilated properly). Or, worst of all, anyone attempting generic, soul-deadening small talk about the weather in a city where the weather was always the same damn oppressive sunshine.

My own attire – thrift-store X-Ray Spex t-shirt faded to a muddy grey, ripped black jeans strategically safety-pinned at the knee, scuffed combat boots that weighed a ton but felt like solid ground beneath my feet – screamed 'financial aid kid trying to remain invisible' louder than any official designation. It was its own kind of uniform, a deliberate, if futile, counterpoint to the casual wealth and logo-heavy conformity surrounding me. *Look closer,* it tried to say. *See the seams. See the struggle.* But nobody ever did.

My pen scratched across the page, finding a vicious satisfaction in capturing Chad's self-satisfied smirk, exaggerating the vacuous gleam in his eyes until he looked like a Ken doll contemplating the crushing weight of his own perfection (or maybe just his next protein shake). Beside him, I drew a meticulously groomed poodle, balancing precariously on its hind legs, wearing a miniature university security cap pulled low over its vacant eyes and holding a tiny, sparking taser. *Campus Paw-trol: Ensuring a Safe & Compliant Learning Environment Since Last Tuesday.*

Someone jostled my arm hard enough to send a jagged line across the poodle's perfectly coiffed head. "Hey, Gem."

It was Rhys, looking flustered from his failed attempt to integrate with Chad's crew. He materialized beside me, leaning against a nearby concrete planter filled with suspiciously drought-resistant flowers, attempting Chad's casual lean but missing the required arrogance by a mile. It just made him look awkward, like he wasn't sure what to do with his hands, which were currently fiddling with the strap of his pristine guitar case. His brand-new, artfully distressed Clash t-shirt (pretty sure it was a reproduction, bought online, probably pre-ripped for that authentic punk look) clashed violently with his clean-cut khakis and spotless white sneakers. He gestured vaguely towards Chad's oblivious group with his phone. "Heard about the curfew? Wild, huh? Ten o'clock, man. Seriously cuts into the night."

"Scintillating," I muttered, trying to erase the errant line without tearing the paper. "Truly, the defining issue of our generation."

"Yeah, well," Rhys shifted his weight, pocketing his phone after a quick, reflexive glance at his screen – checking his reflection, probably, or maybe a notification from one of the mainstream music blogs he followed religiously. "At least it shouldn't mess with band practice too much, right? We usually wrap before then anyway." He was fishing again. For validation, for shared annoyance, for *something*. A sign that we were on the same wavelength, inconvenienced together by the Man.

I gave him a noncommittal grunt, focusing intently on the poodle's fur texture, using tight, angry little circles. Rhys wasn't *bad*. Not really. He could play rhythm guitar okay, mostly kept time, had decent gear (thanks, Dad!), and genuinely seemed to like the *sound* of the music, the energy. But he didn't always get the *point*. It was like he heard the volume but missed the frequency. He was tuned into the city's background static, the official pronouncements, the SNN soundbites, the curated playlists, but the coded warnings underneath, the things left unsaid, the rising tide of *wrongness* – that all seemed to pass him by. He was more focused on saving up for that vintage overdrive pedal, the 'Screaming Eagle 3000' or whatever bullshit name it had, the one supposedly used by Iron Eagle's lead guitarist. He admired their "intensity," their "professional sound," their "killer riffs," somehow managing to ignore the thinly veiled fascist dog whistles woven through their lyrics ("Blood and Soil," "Pure Volition," charming stuff like that) and the stylized SS bolts incorporated into their logo. Oblivious. Or choosing to be. The line blurred more every day, worn thin by convenience and privilege.

"Gotta run," I said, snapping the sketchbook shut before he could angle for a look at the poodle-cop. "Intro to Critical Theory isn't gonna critique itself. Professor Davies actually expects us to deconstruct the dominant paradigm, unlike some people."

He blinked, the reference sailing miles over his perfectly styled hair. "Oh. Right. Critical... yeah. Cool." He offered a vague thumbs-up. "Catch you later, then. Practice tonight?"

"Jessica's texting details," I said, already moving, melting back into the indifferent student tide.

The off-campus apartment I shared with three other strangers – united only by the crushing weight of GLAMA rents and a mutual tolerance for overflowing recycling bins – perpetually smelled like a potent cocktail of stale ramen noodles, someone's cheap synthetic berry-flavoured weed vape (probably Ben's), and the faint, lingering acidic aroma of turpentine and desperation (definitely Chloe's). It wasn't home, not the way Mom and Dad's cramped but familiar house in the Valley still felt like an anchor, however frayed. But this apartment, with its peeling paint and questionable plumbing, was what their second mortgage and my own rapidly accumulating mountain of federal and private loans paid for. A precarious foothold in the glittering, unaffordable, relentlessly consuming metropolis of GLAMA.

I let myself in, the flimsy door lock clicking weakly behind me. The living room, theoretically a common space according to the lease agreement none of us probably read closely enough, had long ago been colonized by Chloe. Her imposing easel stood near the grimy window overlooking a brick wall, surrounded by paint-splattered drop cloths, canvases in various states of completion leaning against the walls, and sticky jars bristling with brushes soaking in murky water. The lumpy sofa, a relic from a previous tenant, was pushed back against the far wall to maximize floor space, draped in yet another stained drop cloth. The only sign anyone else ever acknowledged this room's existence was the large flat-screen TV mounted opposite the sofa, currently tuned, inevitably, to the Sterling News Network. It provided a constant, droning background noise, the video equivalent of beige wallpaper, while Chloe wrestled with her artistic demons. She claimed the "soothing, authoritative voices" helped her concentrate, blocking out the city noise. I thought it was more like slow-acting poison, seeping into the air, coating everything with a thin film of acceptable lies. Mom and Dad watched it too, their anxieties about the future somehow soothed by SNN's carefully curated narratives of stability and strength, even as they fretted about making ends meet.

Tonight's SNN headline crawled across the bottom of the screen, nestled below the gleaming network logo: "GLAMA Authorities Applaud Citizen Cooperation Following Minor Downtown Disturbances; Order Restored." The anchor, a woman with helmet-like hair and an unnervingly fixed smile, was interviewing a uniformed GLAMA PD spokesperson.

Minor disturbances. Right. My stomach tightened. I'd spent half an hour last night glued to a shaky, pixelated livestream on an encrypted channel before the feed abruptly cut – kids my age, younger even, holding cardboard signs scrawled with "Housing Not Handcuffs" and "GLAMA Belongs To Us," protesting the latest impossible rent hikes and summary evictions sweeping through the Eastside barrios. Met by GLAMA PD looking like they'd stepped off the set of some grimdark sci-fi blockbuster, all black composite armor, visored helmets reflecting the streetlights, deploying sonic deterrents and advancing in perfect, terrifying formation. Looked pretty damn major, pretty damn brutal, to me. But here, on SNN, it was just carefully edited footage – wide shots avoiding close-ups of bleeding faces or panicked crowds, calm official voices blaming "professional agitators" and "outside influences," praising the swift "restoration of order." No mention of the armored personnel carriers rolling down residential streets like invading tanks, the clouds of tear gas drifting into apartment windows, the rough arrests, the zip-tied wrists. Just smooth voices, reassuring graphics, and the underlying message: *Don't worry. Don't look too closely. Everything is under control.* Pure narrative management. Sterling's specialty. He didn't just own the network; he owned the narrative.

Chloe glanced up from dabbing cadmium yellow onto a canvas depicting what looked like a screaming toaster caught in a spiderweb. Her own hair was electric blue this week, clipped back messily with binder clips. Paint smudged her cheekbone like a bruise. Art student solidarity only went so far; her parents, wealthy gallery owners, paid her tuition, rent, *and* supply bills without blinking. Our struggles weren't remotely comparable, a fact that hung unspoken in the air between us most of the time. "Hey, Gem," she said, pulling one side of her oversized, noise-canceling headphones off her ear. The tinny beat of hyper-produced, autotuned synth-pop leaked into the room, clashing weirdly with the SNN anchor's drone. "Your mom called earlier. Like, an hour ago? Sounded kinda stressed. Something about needing to confirm your FAFSA details again. Said the portal wasn't working for her? You should probably call her back."

I forced a tight smile, the muscles in my jaw aching from the effort. "Yeah. Totally. Later." Calling Mom. An exercise in conversational Aikido. It meant navigating a carefully constructed minefield of anxieties – hers about my grades ("Are you keeping up, honey? It's such an opportunity, we sacrificed so much!"), my safety ("Are you being careful walking home from those... band things? GLAMA seems so tense lately..."), my questionable life choices ("Are you sure that band thing is... wise? Does it interfere with your studies?"). And mine about her willful, determined denial of how bad things were actually getting outside their carefully curated suburban bubble, her tendency to dismiss my concerns as youthful pessimism or paranoia. It meant manufacturing reassurances I didn't feel ("Everything's fine, Mom, really") and dodging questions I didn't want to answer about the 'minor disturbances' or the creeping dread that felt like smog choking the city half the time. Later. Definitely later. When I had more psychic energy to deflect and weave and lie convincingly. The FAFSA thing was probably just an excuse anyway, a hook to hang her worries on.

Chloe shrugged, already turning back to her screaming toaster, the conversation forgotten, submerged beneath the synth-pop tide. "Okay. Just sayin'." Her headphones clamped back over her ears.

I walked past her makeshift studio, the smell of turpentine sharp in my nostrils, down the narrow, perpetually dim hall toward my room. The doors to the other two bedrooms were closed, as usual. Maya, the aspiring novelist, was probably hunched over her ancient laptop inside hers, chain-smoking herbal cigarettes and writing tortured, semi-autobiographical poetry or screenplays destined to remain unproduced masterpieces.

Ben, the digital arts major, was likely locked in his room, bathed in the glow of multiple monitors, designing VTuber avatars with disturbingly large eyes for questionable clients online, or disappearing entirely into whatever immersive VR game was currently consuming his life and bandwidth. We exchanged occasional grunts over the overflowing trash bins in the kitchen or passive-aggressive notes left on the fridge about dirty dishes, but mostly we coexisted in parallel orbits of solitary pursuits and low-level, simmering anxiety. Definitely not the "found family" the glossy university brochures promised with pictures of laughing, diverse students sharing wholesome meals.

My own door, the one that didn't quite latch unless you slammed it just right, offered the only real sanctuary. I kicked it mostly shut, the warped wood groaning in protest. Inside, it was barely big enough for the second-hand mattress on the floor, the leaning tower of textbooks threatening imminent collapse, and my beat-up Fender Precision bass leaning protectively in the corner like a silent guardian. The worn, cracked Woody Guthrie sticker – "This Machine Kills Fascists" – was peeling determinedly at the edges, a constant battle against humidity and entropy. I smoothed it down again, pressing the curling vinyl back against the scratched black finish. A ritual. A prayer. A joke. Maybe all three in this upside-down, crumbling world.

I flopped onto the mattress, the springs groaning in protest like an old man getting out of a chair, and pulled out my phone. Ignored the red notification bubble indicating the missed call from Mom. Ignored the text alert from my bank cheerfully informing me my balance was approaching single digits. Scrolled straight to the message icon. One new text. Green bubble.

Jessica: Practice @ 7? My garage is free. Bring snacks. <3

A small, genuine smile finally pushed through the gloom, warming something tight and cold in my chest. Jessica. My best friend since that bewildering, alienating orientation week freshman year, the Hendrix-channeling fire to my Marley-dubbed earth. The only person at this sprawling, indifferent university who seemed to speak the same language, even if her dialect was inflected with the easy confidence of someone who'd never had to choose between textbooks and groceries. We'd bonded over shitty campus coffee, a mutual love for The Clash and Bad Brains, and a shared, bewildered amusement at the casual, unexamined wealth that dripped from seemingly everyone else around us. Her version of 'struggling' involved driving a five-year-old hybrid instead of the brand-new electric her parents kept trying to buy her. Still, she *tried* to get it. She listened. And she saw *me*, not just the scholarship stats or the quiet Black girl sketching furiously in the corner. Mostly. That 'mostly' was important. *Jessica's Jones.* My own stupid, secret joke. My jones for Jessica. If she only knew.

Me: K. Will bring lint-covered crackers from bottom of backpack & righteous fury.

Jessica: My favorite. Don't forget the fury.

I tossed the phone onto the thin blanket and reached for my bass, the cool, worn wood familiar in my hands. Plugged my headphones into my battered practice amp, the connection crackling slightly – static, always static. Twisted the volume knob just enough to feel it vibrate through the cheap particleboard floor.

For a moment, I just held the instrument, letting the silence in the room settle. Then, my fingers found the strings, not consciously seeking a song, but letting the day's accumulated grit and anxiety start to bleed out. It wasn't the driving rhythm of our usual stuff, not the yearning ska beat of "Free to Be." This was slower, heavier. A low, pulsing E, thick and resonant like a heartbeat in the dark. Then a dissonant slide up the neck, a questioning phrase hanging in the air before resolving back to that root note, that anchor.

I closed my eyes, picturing the quad – the bright banners, the oblivious chatter, Chad's smug face. The bassline shifted, became more agitated, a nervous, syncopated rhythm tapped out against the E string, like footsteps trying to run on uneven pavement. *Safety.* The word echoed in my head, and a discordant chord jumped out under my fingers, ugly and jarring. *Whose safety?*

Then, thinking of Rhys, his easy dismissal, his admiration for Iron Eagle's hollow noise, the rhythm fractured, stumbled, became simpler, almost childishly naive for a bar or two, before catching itself with another low, rumbling pulse. The sound of willful ignorance.

The SNN broadcast flickered behind my eyelids – the smooth anchor, the carefully edited violence. The bassline grew heavier still, descending, a slow, mournful dub pattern, notes spaced far apart, leaving room for the echoes, the lies, the things unseen. A ghost note tapped where a scream should be.

Finally, Jessica's text. The thought of her, the garage, the potential energy of playing *together* – it shifted the mood again. The tempo picked up slightly, the minor key brightened just a fraction, a hint of the defiant ska upstroke sneaking in, a question mark turning into an exclamation point. It wasn't a full song, just fragments, sketches in sound, the musical equivalent of the doodles filling my notebook. Processing the static, trying to find the signal underneath. Trying to find the fury Jessica wanted me to bring. It was in there, somewhere, waiting for the right beat to set it loose.

CHAPTER 2: GEMINI

Jessica lived in one of those sprawling, vaguely Spanish-style houses nestled in the hills overlooking the smog-choked basin of GLAMA. The kind with terracotta roof tiles, perfectly manicured drought-resistant landscaping (a recent, expensive concession to the water crisis), and probably a panic room somewhere. Her parents were dentists to the moderately famous, and their three-car garage was bigger than my entire apartment. It was also, thankfully, mostly soundproofed and filled with top-of-the-line gear Jessica barely seemed to register as exceptional.

I navigated my sputtering, ancient Sterling Model Wee! – affectionately nicknamed "The Rustbucket" despite its mostly plastic body – through the winding hillside roads, the contrast between this neighborhood and my own was jarring, as always. It was an early-generation electric, bought third-hand, with cracked solar panels on the roof that barely held a charge and software so outdated it had already been jailbroken multiple times before I even got it. The irony of driving a Sterling vehicle, even a crappy, obsolete one, wasn't lost on me. Here, the Sterling Security™ lawn signs were discreet, tasteful bronze plaques instead of the aggressive plastic monstrosities common closer to the city center. Surveillance cameras were hidden in tasteful faux-rock formations or tucked under Spanish tile eaves, not bolted nakedly to streetlights like robotic vultures. Even oppression had better aesthetics up here. The air smelled faintly of night-blooming jasmine and chlorine from unseen swimming pools instead of exhaust fumes and desperation (though The Rustbucket occasionally emitted a worrying electrical burning smell).

I parked The Rustbucket a block away, partly out of habit (its battery indicator was notoriously unreliable, and I didn't want to get stranded needing a tow from their pristine driveway) and partly because pulling up in the dented, wheezing electric clown car felt like announcing my otherness too loudly. Slinging my bass case over my shoulder and grabbing the bag of slightly crushed saltines, I walked up the gently sloping driveway, the expensive imported gravel crunching under my boots.

The garage door was already open, spilling warm yellow light and the chaotic, familiar sounds of tuning instruments onto the twilight air. Stepping inside felt like crossing a threshold into the only part of my life that made sense anymore, the only place the static seemed to recede, replaced by a different kind of noise – our noise. The space smelled comfortingly of dusty amplifiers, old wood, ozone from the electronics, and Jessica's faint, expensive-perfume-mixed-with-guitar-polish scent. Posters of punk and reggae legends – The Clash, Bad Brains, Bob Marley, Poly Styrene, X-Ray Spex – were taped haphazardly over the pristine white walls, a small, shared rebellion against the sterile perfection of the house beyond the garage door.

Jessica was already there, hunched over her cherry-red Les Paul, coaxing controlled feedback from a massive Marshall stack with the intense concentration she usually reserved for quantum physics problem sets or mastering a particularly tricky guitar solo. Her dark hair fell across her face, hiding the nervous energy I knew was probably making her chew on her lower lip. She looked up as I came in, her expression clearing into that genuine, relieved smile that always hit me right in the chest, bypassing all my usual defenses. "Gem! Finally. Thought you got lost in the wilds of the Valley."

"Nah, just had to coax The Rustbucket up the hill," I said, dropping my case and cracker bag. "Its guidance system kept trying to reroute me to the nearest Sterling™ charging station, even though I told it not to. Damn thing threatened to go into low-power mode halfway up if I didn't sing it show tunes." I dropped my case and the cracker bag near the battered but comfortable couch shoved against one wall.

Rhys was already set up in his usual spot, meticulously wiping down his gleaming white Stratocaster with a microfiber cloth like he was polishing a holy relic. He nodded a greeting, already plugged in, fingers twitching, itching to play. "Hey, Gem. Ready to rock?" His enthusiasm, as usual, felt slightly forced, slightly too loud, like he was playing the part of 'punk rock guitarist' from a movie he'd seen. He launched into a fast, technically decent but somewhat generic rock riff he'd probably been practicing all week, looking over at Jessica and me for approval. Jessica gave a quick, distracted nod, still tweaking her amp settings. I just grunted, pulling my bass out. Leo, however, ever enthusiastic about pure sound, gave him an appreciative, "Yeah, man, killer tone!" Rhys beamed, satisfied.

"Born ready, Rhys," I deadpanned, pulling my trusty Precision bass from its case, the familiar weight settling comfortably against my hip.

And then there were the others, the essential anchors to our chaotic sound, the rest of Jessica's Jones.

Mack sat behind her drum kit – a beautiful vintage Ludwig set, maple finish glowing warmly under the track lighting, a kit she'd somehow acquired and kept in immaculate condition – methodically tightening a cymbal stand wing nut with the focused, economical precision of someone disarming a bomb. Or maybe assembling one.

Her expression was calm, unreadable, as always, her gaze steady. Slightly older than the rest of us, maybe mid-twenties, she was a grad student over at GLAMA State downtown – the big, sprawling public university Jessica's parents kept trying (and failing) to convince her to transfer to – studying something practical and necessary like urban planning or public policy on the GI Bill.

She rarely spoke unless something actually needed saying, but her presence was grounding, her drumming the solid, unwavering heartbeat beneath our noise. She'd joined six months ago after our last drummer flaked out three days before a crucial gig, answering a cryptic flyer Jessica had posted at a dusty independent record store.

Mack never talked about her past – the rumour, pieced together from overheard fragments and intuition, was Marines, maybe Army Infantry, something involving heavy machinery, desert heat, and seeing things she definitely didn't want to talk about – but she played drums like it was therapy, a way to channel intensity into creation instead of destruction. Her rhythm was impeccable, steady as a rock, sometimes infused with complex, syncopated patterns that hinted at a discipline learned far away from any music school syllabus. She just watched, listened, absorbed the room's energy, and laid down the perfect beat, a quiet storm in the eye of our hurricane. She had this way of setting up her kit, every piece perfectly aligned, every wingnut tightened to the exact same torque, that spoke of ingrained discipline.

Across from her, Leo bounced lightly on the balls of his feet, polishing his trumpet with a soft cloth until it gleamed under the garage lights.

He wore his usual bright, slightly mismatched clothes – a vibrant yellow t-shirt with a cartoon bird on it clashing cheerfully with faded green cargo pants and bright red sneakers.

His energy was infectious, a necessary counterweight to Mack's stoicism and my own default cynicism, but underneath the upbeat ska enthusiasm, I sensed a hidden current. Something harder, sharper. He never talked about the full weight of what happened when he got swept up in that protest downtown last year – the arrest, the fingerprinting, the hours in holding. If you asked, he'd just shrug it off with a forced joke, saying, 'Occupational hazard for a wannabe revolutionary, eh?' or 'You guys wouldn't get it, it's a long story.' But the way his eyes would go distant, the way his usual bright energy would dim for a moment before he forced it back, hinted at a deeper pain he kept locked away. He was Canadian, his family safe back in Toronto, but *he* was here in GLAMA on a student visa that felt increasingly precarious. Whispers about changing regulations, expired clauses suddenly being enforced, other international students getting caught in bureaucratic nets and quietly deported – Leo heard them all, and I knew that prior arrest had put him squarely on someone's list.

That direct taste of state brutality, the constant vulnerability of his status – *that* fueled his passionate belief in resistance, his impatience with caution or coded messages. "No time for coded whispers, Gem," he'd said once, his eyes dark with an intensity that belied his usual easy grin. "Gotta shout it loud while we still can. Before they figure out a way to shut us all up for good."

"Alright," Jessica said, straightening up and slinging her Les Paul over her shoulder, the movement fluid and practiced. "Let's run 'Free to Be' first? Get warmed up?"

Rhys nodded eagerly, already launching into the opening guitar riff, maybe a little too fast, a little too clean. I exchanged a quick glance with Jessica – a silent acknowledgment of Rhys's perpetual eagerness, a shared moment of understanding that still felt easy, natural, despite the growing static around us.

Mack clicked her sticks together – one, two, three, four – a sharp, definitive sound cutting through the lingering amp hum, and the garage exploded with sound. Leo's trumpet soared over Jessica's driving guitar chords, bright and hopeful, a melody full of yearning. Rhys locked into the rhythm, grinning, head bobbing. I found the bass groove, a simple, pulsing reggae beat that felt like the song's hidden heart, the steady counterpoint to the upbeat ska-punk surface.

We played. And for a few minutes, the world outside – the curfews, the scanners, the SNN lies, the anxieties about money and moms and visas and the creeping, suffocating fear – faded into the background, drowned out by the glorious, messy, life-affirming noise we made together. This felt real. This felt necessary.

Leo took a solo, sharp and clear, full of playful energy but with an undercurrent of defiance I could hear even if Rhys couldn't. Rhys, catching the simpler surface vibe, grinned and mirrored a couple of Leo's phrases on his guitar, a flash of genuine musical connection that transcended his usual awkwardness. He glanced over at me, looking for approval, a quick, hopeful flicker in his eyes, and this time I gave him a small, genuine nod. He beamed, hitting the next chord with extra enthusiasm. See? Not bad. Just… incomplete. Listening, but not hearing.

As the song built towards the final chorus, I stepped up to the mic, letting my voice join in, singing the lines I'd written late one night, thinking about the walls closing in, thinking about Jessica, thinking about the simple, impossible desire to just *be*.

"Don't you wanna be free to be? Just free to be, authentically? Who you are behind the mask / Is that too much for us to ask?"

The words felt different singing them here, in this safe space, surrounded by my band, my chosen family. Hopeful, almost. A declaration whispered inside a shout. But the last line caught in my throat, the question hanging heavy in the suddenly quiet air as the final chord faded. "What are we waitin' for?"

The song crashed to an end. Silence rang in the garage, thick and sudden, charged with unspoken things.

"Yeah!" Rhys pumped his fist, oblivious as ever to the undercurrents. "Nailed it! That felt tight."

Leo wiped his mouthpiece, nodding slowly. "Good energy. Good warm-up." His eyes held a question, though, watching Jessica, perhaps sensing something wasn't quite right.

Mack just gave a single, almost imperceptible nod from behind the drum kit, her gaze resting on Jessica for a beat longer than usual, observant as always.

Jessica pushed her hair back, avoiding my gaze now, her eyes finding a sudden fascination with the scuffed toe of her expensive boot. She offered a small, tight smile that didn't quite reach her eyes. "Yeah," she said, her voice a little too bright, a little too quick. "Yeah, it was good. Solid." I saw it clearly – the flicker of panic behind the forced casualness. The song's plea for authenticity had scraped against the smooth surface of the mask she wore, the one designed to meet her parents' expectations, to fit neatly into the world Sterling was building, the one that kept her own complicated feelings safely locked away. She wasn't ready to face what the song stirred up, not yet. And I wouldn't push. I'd written the song for her, about her, about *us*, but she had to be the one to unlock the door. I could wait.

"Okay," I said, deliberately breaking the fragile tension, needing to keep moving, keep playing before the silence allowed those unspoken things to solidify. I adjusted the strap on my bass, the worn leather familiar against my shoulder. "Let's try 'Torn to Shreds.' And Rhys? Try to keep the tempo steady this time. Feel the pocket."

He flushed slightly at the implied criticism but nodded, eager to please, already adjusting his stance. Mack counted us in again, sharp and precise – one, two, three, four – and the noise started once more, a different energy this time, angrier, faster, pushing back the silence, pushing back the fear. For now.

The drive to the gig was tense, thick with unspoken anxieties. We were playing downtown, at The Rat Hole, a legendary dive bar tucked away on a grimy side street, known for its perpetually sticky floors, questionable plumbing that occasionally backed up mid-set, and a surprisingly decent sound system salvaged from some defunct rock club. It was also known for attracting a mixed, volatile crowd – dedicated punks in faded battle vests, curious university students slumming it, intense-looking activists handing out zines, local musicians checking out the scene, and occasionally, less savory elements drawn to the scene's raw, confrontational energy like moths to a flickering, dangerous flame. Getting there meant navigating GLAMA's increasingly fractured landscape, crossing invisible lines between zones of curated safety and neglected reality. The route Jessica usually took felt different tonight; more GLAMA PD cruisers visible, their blue lights casting an unsettling glow. One street we often cut through was blocked off entirely, a couple of officers standing guard, their faces impassive. "Detour," Jessica muttered, her voice tight, taking a longer way around.

I noticed some freshly painted-over graffiti on a wall near an overpass – a crude anti-Sterling slogan I'd seen just last week, now just a meaningless grey smudge. The city felt like it was holding its breath.

We'd crammed ourselves and our gear into Jessica's parents' gleaming white minivan – the 'sensible' vehicle they insisted she drive instead of her own beat-up but beloved hybrid when venturing into "less desirable" parts of the city, like anywhere south of Wilshire or east of the river. The irony wasn't lost on me, sitting in the plush leather seats surrounded by state-of-the-art safety features, heading to play anti-establishment anthems in a bar called The Rat Hole. Jessica drove, her knuckles white on the expensive steering wheel, navigating the choked freeway traffic with a tense precision that betrayed her nerves. Mack rode shotgun, silent as usual, but her eyes constantly scanned the road, the other cars, the overpasses – her usual quiet vigilance dialed up to eleven tonight. Leo, Rhys, and I were crammed in the back amidst amps smelling faintly of ozone, Mack's neatly packed drum hardware cases, and the lingering scent of Jessica's dad's expensive air freshener.

"Did you see those new checkpoints near the Seventh Street bridge?" Leo asked, peering out the tinted window as we merged onto the congested 101 freeway. Traffic slowed to a crawl. "Looks like full GLAMA PD, tactical gear and everything, not just traffic cops. Saw them pulling over older cars, looked like profiling to me."

Rhys, absorbed in scrolling through some music gear forum on his phone, mumbled without looking up, "Probably just checking for curfew violations. Gotta keep things orderly, right? Like that SNN report said."

Leo shot him a look sharp enough to cut glass across the confined space of the minivan. "Orderly? Or compliant? There's a difference, Rhys."

"Whoa, man, just saying what they said on the news," Rhys said defensively, finally looking up, sensing the sudden chill in the air. "They said it was about stopping trouble before it starts."

"Maybe don't believe everything you hear on Sterling News?" I muttered, leaning my head against the vibrating window, the low thrum of the engine mingling with the tension. The city slid past outside the tinted glass – gleaming corporate towers downtown scraped the hazy sky, giving way abruptly to neglected industrial zones with broken windows and rusting fences, then suddenly gentrified blocks where trendy minimalist cafes selling $8 lattes stood next to boarded-up storefronts plastered with eviction notices. The contrasts felt sharper lately, the edges harder, the buffer zones shrinking. Patches of vibrant, angry street art I remembered seeing just months ago were painted over with dull, municipal grey or replaced by bland, regime-approved "public art" installations featuring abstract shapes and soothing corporate colors. More cameras seemed to sprout from every pole and building corner, their dark, smoked-glass lenses like the unblinking eyes of predatory insects. *It wasn't always like this,* a voice whispered in my head, insistent. *Or maybe it was, and I just wasn't paying enough attention before.* Maybe the boiling frog analogy was real.

We finally exited the freeway into the warehouse district surrounding The Rat Hole. The streets were darker here, narrower, hemmed in by tall brick buildings stained with decades of grime. The air here was thick with the smell of diesel fumes, stagnant water from clogged storm drains, and the faint, sweetish odor of decay. Fewer official cameras, maybe, but more watchful eyes from shadowy doorways and fire escapes. We passed a wall plastered with layers of peeling flyers – some for bands playing long-forgotten gigs, some grainy photos seeking missing persons ("Have You Seen Maria? Last Seen Near 5th St."), some bearing the stark, crossed-out logo of a local anti-fascist action group. Someone had spray-painted "FUCK STERLING" in jagged red letters across a boarded-up pawn shop window, but it was already partially, sloppily painted over in municipal grey, the message still visible underneath like a stubborn scar.

"Place looks sketchier than usual," Jessica murmured, her voice tight, slowing the van as we approached the dimly lit entrance to the club. A small group loitered near the door under the flickering neon sign depicting a cartoon rat playing a guitar. They were dressed mostly in black, some with shaved heads or heavy boots, their postures radiating a low-level, coiled menace. Not the usual mix of punk scene regulars. They had the same aggressive look as the Iron Eagle fans I'd seen at other gigs, the ones who always seemed more interested in starting trouble than listening to music.

"Iron Eagle fans?" Leo asked quietly from the back seat, his voice tight with recognition. "Or just... fans of intimidation?"

Mack just grunted, her eyes fixed on the group, assessing. "Stay alert. Load in fast."

We pulled into the narrow, garbage-strewn alley behind the club, the designated load-in zone. The air here smelled powerfully of stale beer, overflowing dumpsters leaking suspicious fluids, and old urine. Charming. As we started wrestling our heavy gear out of the minivan's pristine cargo space, the dented metal back door of the club creaked open and Sal, the club's owner – a grizzled punk survivor with faded tattoos covering his arms and more gaps than teeth in his weary smile – stuck his head out.

"Jessica's Jones! 'Bout time," he rasped, his voice like gravel scraping concrete. He wiped his hands on a greasy apron stretched tight over his faded Ramones t-shirt. "Listen up. Keep it tight tonight, okay? No bullshit. GLAMA PD has been sniffing around all week, citing phantom noise ordinances, checking permits like they're looking for contraband. They shut down The Pit last week over a supposed fire code violation nobody ever heard of before, conveniently right before that big anti-Sterling benefit show. Funny how that works." He sighed, running a hand over his bald head. "Keep your set clean, finish on time, no political rants from the stage, got it? I can't afford the heat. They find one excuse, they'll shut me down for good." He looked genuinely stressed, the usual defiant spark in his eyes dimmed by exhaustion and worry. Another freedom chipped away, I thought bitterly. The freedom to be loud, to be messy, to piss people off, to even exist if you weren't making the right noises for the right people. The shrinking space for dissent was palpable.

"We got it, Sal," Jessica assured him, though her voice wavered slightly.

"Yeah," Sal grunted, eyeing our gear skeptically. "Just... be cool. Don't give 'em an excuse." He disappeared back inside, the door slamming shut with a final-sounding thud.

We hauled our amps and drums through the narrow doorway into the club's sticky embrace, the tension from the street and Sal's warning clinging to us like the alley grime. The club interior was dark, cavernous, already filling up with a mix of familiar faces from the scene and wary-looking strangers, including a few more who looked like the group outside. The air thrummed with low, anxious conversation and the bass-heavy throb of whatever opening band was sound-checking on the small, sticker-covered stage. It felt different from the polished sterility of the university campus, charged with a raw energy that was equal parts exciting and dangerous. This was where the real music happened. Or used to.

Backstage – which was really just a cramped, graffiti-scarred storage room smelling powerfully of mildew, stale cigarette smoke, and nervous sweat – the mood was subdued, brittle. Rhys fussed over tuning his guitar, his earlier enthusiasm replaced by a frown of concentration. Leo paced back and forth, running scales on his trumpet, the notes sharp and anxious. Mack sat on an overturned milk crate, methodically arranging her drumsticks on a towel laid across a dusty amp case, her face impassive but her shoulders tight. Jessica leaned against the crumbling plaster wall, chewing her lip, her eyes darting nervously towards the door leading to the main room. I leaned against a stack of empty kegs that smelled faintly of vomit, pulling out my sketchbook, needing the familiar scratch of pen on paper, needing to capture the nervous energy, the grime, the feeling of being underground, literally and figuratively, waiting for the signal to begin.

Tonight, "Free to Be" felt less like a personal confession and more like a necessary invocation. A fragile shield against the encroaching darkness. A plea for some kind of authentic space in a world determined to pave it all over with compliance and fear. I took a deep breath, the air thick with anticipation and something that might have been fear, but felt suspiciously like hope, sharp and dangerous. We were up next.

CHAPTER 3:
JESSICA LAMAS

The final chord of "Free to Be" crashed and echoed in the humid, beer-soaked air of The Rat Hole. For a second, there was just the ringing in my ears, the thumping of my own heart against my ribs, and the smell of sweat – mine, the band's, the packed crowd's. A thick, pungent miasma of human exertion, cheap beer, and something vaguely like mildew. Then, the applause hit, not a polite ripple but a genuine wave of sound washing over the small stage, mixed with whoops and a few appreciative whistles from the darkness beyond the lights. It wasn't a stadium roar, not the kind of adulation I sometimes daydreamed about, but here, in this grimy, beloved dive, it felt electric. Real. Earned.

My fingers ached slightly from gripping the neck of my Les Paul, the familiar smooth wood suddenly feeling foreign. I'd almost fumbled the bridge, my concentration wavering for just a beat. Gemini's lyrics... sometimes they felt less like words and more like tiny, sharp probes digging under my skin. That line, "Who you are behind the mask / Is that too much for us to ask?" It snagged on something inside me, a hook catching on fabric I didn't know was frayed. The glare of the cheap stage lights felt too bright, too revealing. I pushed the feeling down, hard, focusing instead on the technical execution of the song just finished – the satisfying crunch of the power chords, the smooth transition into the solo, the clean fingerpicking on the outro. *Stay focused, Jess. Play the part. Be the rockstar.*

Rhys pumped his fist beside me, grinning ear-to-ear, sweat plastering his bangs to his forehead. He soaked up the applause like a thirsty plant, turning slightly to acknowledge a whoop from the crowd. Leo gave a quick, flashy bow from the knee, trumpet held high like a trophy, ever the showman, playing to the back rows even though there probably weren't any.

Mack, almost invisible behind the drum kit except for the glint of light off her cymbal, offered only the slightest, almost imperceptible nod to the crowd, already adjusting the angle of her snare drum, her face impassive. And Gemini...

Gemini just stood there beside the mic stand she shared with me, bass held low against her hip, her expression unreadable as she surveyed the room. Her eyes, dark and steady, seemed to absorb everything – the peeling paint on the walls, the flickering neon beer signs, the faces in the crowd, the tension coiling in the corners. That quiet intensity of hers could be unnerving. Sometimes I felt like she could see right through the carefully constructed walls I kept around myself, the ones labeled 'good daughter,' 'talented musician,' 'well-adjusted student.' I quickly looked away, busying myself with checking my tuning pegs, needing a task, a physical anchor. The applause felt good, validating, proof that we didn't suck, but that brief moment of vulnerability the song evoked left me feeling exposed, unsteady on the sticky stage floor.

"Alright!" I leaned into my mic, forcing brightness into my voice. "Thanks, you guys are awesome! This next one's called 'Torn to Shreds'!"

Gemini gave me a quick, questioning glance – *Are you okay?* – but I just nodded curtly, signaling Mack. Mack's sticks clicked – one, two, three, *four* – and we launched into the next song, the faster tempo and angrier lyrics a welcome relief, something I could pour energy into without thinking too hard. The crowd surged forward again, a small, sweaty mosh pit erupting near the front, bodies colliding in a chaotic, joyful release. This was familiar territory, the raw energy exchange I loved. Playing music, losing myself in the sound, the intricate patterns of the fretboard under my fingers – it was the only time the constant low-level hum of anxiety and expectation truly faded. The only time I felt... well, almost free.

"Good set, kids. Real good." Sal cornered us as we came off stage, wiping condensation from a bottle of water onto his already damp apron. His usual cynical squint was softened slightly. "You got 'em moving. Especially with that last one." He jerked his head towards the stage, where the next band was already setting up. "Just... maybe watch the volume on that one next time? Sounded like you were trying to bring the damn roof down. And the moshing got a little hairy near the end there." He glanced nervously towards the front door, where a couple of GLAMA PD cruisers had slowly rolled past mid-set, their blue and red lights momentarily painting the grimy windows. "Don't need any excuses for them to come knocking, y'know?"

"Sorry, Sal," I said quickly. "Got a little carried away."

"Yeah, well, energy's good," he conceded gruffly. "Just... controlled energy, alright? Keep it smart." He clapped Leo on the shoulder. "Nice horn work, kid." Then he bustled off towards the bar, already scanning the crowd for trouble.

We started breaking down our gear, the post-show adrenaline slowly ebbing, replaced by weariness and the slightly sticky feeling of dried sweat. The backstage room felt even smaller and grimier now.

"He's right, though," Rhys said, carefully coiling his cables. "That pit was getting pretty intense. Saw some dude almost lose an eye."

"That's punk rock, Rhys," Leo said, carefully packing his trumpet into its case. "Sometimes you gotta risk an eye to feel something real."

"Or maybe just avoid concussion," Mack murmured, efficiently dismantling her snare stand with practiced movements. It was the most she'd said all night.

As we started hauling amps towards the back alley door, a knot of guys blocked the narrow exit. They were the ones from outside earlier, dressed in black, boots heavy, faces set in sullen lines. One of them, taller than the rest, with a faded 'Iron Eagle' patch barely visible on his bomber jacket, stepped forward, deliberately bumping into Leo.

"Watch it, horn boy," he sneered, his eyes flicking dismissively over Leo's bright clothes.

Leo bristled instantly, stepping forward, his easygoing vibe vanishing. "Maybe watch where you're going, *fass-cista*." He practically spat the last word.

The guy's friends tensed, hands clenching. My heart hammered against my ribs. This was exactly what Sal warned us about. Rhys took an involuntary step back, eyes wide. Gemini moved forward slightly, placing herself beside Leo, her hand resting almost casually on the neck of her bass like it was a weapon.

Before anyone else could move or speak, Mack materialized silently beside the tall guy. She didn't say a word, just stood there, solid and immovable, her gaze level and utterly devoid of fear. She wasn't overtly threatening, but there was something in her stillness, in the way she occupied the space, that radiated pure, undiluted *competence*. Like she could dismantle him as efficiently as she dismantled her drum kit. The guy met her gaze for a split second, seemed to register something that made him uncomfortable, and then sneered again, but with less conviction. "Whatever. Move it." He shoved past Mack, his shoulder brushing hers, followed by his friends, and disappeared out into the alley.

The tension broke, leaving a shaky silence.

"Assholes," Leo muttered, rubbing his shoulder where the guy had bumped him.

"You okay?" I asked him, my voice a little breathless.

He nodded, his jaw tight. "Yeah. Fine. Just... tired of them."

"Good job, Mack," Gemini said quietly, giving Mack a respectful nod.

Mack just shrugged, picking up a cymbal case. "Load out," she said, her voice flat. Back to business. We were a team, alright. A weird, fractured, barely-holding-it-together team, but maybe that counted for something. We finished packing the minivan in tense silence, the earlier exhilaration of the performance completely gone, replaced by the sour taste of the city's ugliness.

The next morning, the contrast was, as always, jarring. Back home in the quiet, sun-drenched hills, the chaos and confrontation of The Rat Hole felt like a distant, slightly unbelievable dream. Our house, all clean lines, muted earth tones, and expensive, vaguely abstract art, smelled faintly of lemon polish and my mother's imported Japanese green tea. No overflowing dumpsters or stale cigarette smoke here. Just orderly calm and the low hum of the air conditioning fighting the GLAMA heat.

I sat at the polished granite island in the kitchen, nursing a mug of artisanal coffee from a local roaster Mom favored, pretending to study the intricate molecular structures for my O-Chem midterm on my tablet. Outside the panoramic window, automatic sprinklers hissed across the impossibly green lawn – a defiant, resource-intensive display against GLAMA's perpetual drought warnings and rationing notices that didn't seem to apply up here. My father sat opposite me, already dressed in his crisp, light blue dental scrubs, scrolling through headlines on his own tablet – the latest, sleekest Sterling™ model, naturally. He always had the newest Sterling tech; claimed it streamlined his practice management.

"Morning, mija," he said without looking up from his screen. "Sleep well?"

"Fine, Dad." Standard answer. No need to mention getting home after 1 AM, reeking of dive bar and adrenaline, the encounter in the alley replaying in my head.

"Good, good." He took a delicate sip of his espresso. "Saw an interesting piece on the Sterling feed this morning. They're launching a big city-wide initiative. 'Freedom's Ring.' Some kind of music competition for local talent. Big prize money, national exposure on SNN. Sterling himself is backing it." He scrolled further down the article. "Says here he wants to 'give back to the community,' foster 'positive creative outlets' for the city's youth." He finally looked up, a thoughtful, appraising expression on his face. "Sounds like quite the opportunity for a band like yours. You know, your mother mentioned that Mrs. Anderson – Rick Anderson's wife, you know, the producer at Sterling Entertainment? Apparently, she's a patient of mine now, lovely woman – was saying how much Mr. Sterling enjoys supporting young, harmonious artists. Could be a real advantage, Jess."

My stomach gave a weird little lurch, a confused mix of interest and unease. Sterling. *Freedom's Ring.* The name itself felt like cynical branding, like something cooked up in a marketing meeting to sound inspiring while serving some other purpose. Everything Sterling touched seemed designed to consolidate his power, polish his increasingly controversial image, or push his vaguely authoritarian, hyper-capitalist agenda. His media outlets were notorious for their biased reporting, drowning out other perspectives. His tech company built the surveillance systems watching the city. A music competition backed by *him*? It sounded... suspicious. Calculated. Like something Gemini would immediately dissect as a propaganda exercise wrapped in a shiny package. The word "harmonious," especially coming indirectly from someone connected to Sterling Entertainment, echoed unpleasantly.

And yet. *National exposure. Big prize money.* The words snagged in my mind, appealing to a part of me I didn't like to acknowledge – the part that craved validation beyond the sticky floors of The Rat Hole, the part that felt the constant, unspoken weight of my parents' expectations (prestigious university, successful career, marry someone 'suitable'), the part that secretly wondered if maybe, just maybe, our band could actually *be* something more. The part that felt a twinge of guilt about the advantages I already had, and the conflicting desire to prove I deserved them, or could achieve something beyond them on my own terms. This felt like a shortcut, a potential fast track. An 'advantage', as Dad would call it.

"Huh," I said, trying to sound casual, turning my tablet away from O-Chem diagrams to search for 'Freedom's Ring GLAMA'. The official site popped up instantly – slick graphics, soaring, vaguely patriotic background music, professionally shot photos of diverse, smiling young musicians (none of whom looked remotely punk or angry), and Sterling's benevolent, carefully airbrushed face beaming from the corner like a digital saint. "Unleash Your Voice! Celebrate GLAMA!" the headline screamed. It felt... slick. Corporate. Manipulative, probably. Gemini would hate it on sight.

But the prize package... it was significant. Professional studio time, new gear endorsements (imagine telling Rhys!), a guaranteed slot opening for a major touring act (probably one signed to Sterling's affiliated label), and, of course, the SNN broadcast feature. Enough to make a real difference. Enough to maybe get us out of my parents' garage and Sal's back alley for good. Enough to maybe make my parents see the band as something more than a noisy hobby.

"Maybe... maybe we should check it out?" The words were out before I could stop them, sounding hesitant even to my own ears. Was I betraying something just by considering it?

Dad smiled, that proud, slightly condescending smile he got when he thought I was finally thinking practically, strategically, like him. "That's my girl. Always looking for the angle. It could be a fantastic platform. Networking opportunities, too. You never know who might be watching. Important people go to these things." He finished his espresso in one gulp and stood up, patting my shoulder. "Gotta run. Cavities wait for no man. Think about it, Jess. Could be big."

He left, leaving me alone in the sun-drenched, silent kitchen with the slick propaganda website glowing on my tablet screen and a growing knot of conflict tightening in my gut. Opportunity? Or trap? Or maybe, just maybe, both?

"Absolutely not." Gemini didn't even look up from meticulously cleaning her bass strings with a worn grey rag. We were back in the garage a few days later, the air thick with the smell of stale crackers and amp ozone. Her voice was flat, final.

I'd barely gotten the words "Freedom's Ring" out of my mouth. I took a breath, trying again. "But Gem, just listen to the prize package–"

"I don't need to hear the prize package, Jess," she interrupted, still focused on her bass. "It's sponsored by Sterling Corp, broadcast exclusively on Sterling News Network. It's a propaganda machine wearing a battle-of-the-bands costume. It's literally everything we supposedly stand against."

"But the exposure!" Rhys chimed in immediately, predictably latching onto the shiniest part. He leaned forward from the battered couch where he'd been scrolling on his phone, eyes bright with ambition. "National TV! Think about it! People would actually *hear* us! We could get a record deal, better gear... maybe even tour!" He trailed off, practically vibrating with excitement.

"Exactly," Gemini said, her voice dangerously quiet. She stopped polishing and finally looked up, pinning Rhys with a look that could freeze lava. "They *want* people to hear us – playing *their* game, on *their* stage, validating *their* whole rotten system just by showing up. They'll control the narrative, edit the footage, make us look like happy little cogs in Sterling's 'Unity Through Excellence' machine while they cut away from any lyric that actually says something." She shifted her gaze to me, her dark eyes intense. "Don't you see it, Jess? It's a trap. A gilded cage, maybe, but still a cage."

I shifted uncomfortably on the overturned amp I was using as a stool. I *did* see it. Or at least, I saw why *she* saw it that way. Her view was always sharper, less forgiving. But the lure of the prize, the thought of maybe, finally, getting some real recognition, of proving something to my parents, to myself... it was strong. It felt like a chance, maybe the only one we'd get, to break out. "Maybe," I said carefully, testing the waters, avoiding Gemini's direct gaze, "maybe we could subvert it? Use their platform against them? What if we played 'Static Scream' live on SNN?" That was one of our angriest, most chaotic songs, full of feedback and Gemini's most biting lyrics. Surely *that* couldn't be co-opted.

Leo, who'd been quietly doing breathing exercises with his trumpet mouthpiece, lowered it, his expression thoughtful. "The platform *is* tempting, Gem," he admitted, rubbing his chin. "Hard to reach people, spread the real message, from alleys like Sal's. We need bigger stages if we want to wake people up." He caught Gemini's deeply skeptical look. "Maybe... maybe Jess has a point? If we're smart about it? Go in with eyes open?" He paused, the ever-present vulnerability flickering in his eyes. "Or maybe it *is* a trap. Maybe it's too dangerous, especially for... for some of us."

Mack, leaning back against her silent drum kit, just watched us, tapping a complex, syncopated rhythm on her knee with a single drumstick. Assessing. Waiting. Her silence was often louder than our arguments.

"Subvert it?" Gemini snorted, the sound full of derision. She turned back to her bass, plucking a low, discordant note. "How, Jess? By playing slightly angrier lyrics while they sandwich us between some vapid synth-pop drones and a folk band singing about how great GLAMA is? They'll drown us in patriotic B-roll and cut to commercial before we finish the first verse if they don't like what they hear. It's naive to think we can beat them at their own game on their own turf. They *own* the turf."

"So we just keep playing The Rat Hole forever?" Rhys demanded, his voice rising in frustration. "Never try to actually get anywhere? Never try to win?"

"Winning isn't the point, Rhys!" Gemini shot back, finally standing up, her quiet intensity replaced by a flash of fire. "Playing The Rat Hole *means* something! Playing outside their system, building our own thing, *that's* the point! This competition... it's poison. It's designed to co-opt dissent, sanitize it, make it safe and marketable for Sterling's sponsors, or crush it if it won't comply. And we'd be walking right into it, asking them to please poison us, just for a chance at maybe getting slightly better gear?"

The air crackled with tension. Rhys looked mutinous. Leo looked conflicted. Mack looked... watchful. I felt caught in the middle, pulled between Gemini's stark, unforgiving clarity and Rhys's simple, understandable ambition, between Leo's cautious idealism and my own confusing mix of fear and desire. Part of me desperately wanted Gemini to be wrong, wanted the 'opportunity' to be real, a clean shot. Another part knew deep down that she was probably right. It felt compromised, slick, dangerous in a way that had nothing to do with mosh pits or sketchy alleys. The argument stalled, hanging heavy in the garage air. Gemini wouldn't budge.

Later that week, I found Gemini alone, sketching by the dubious "wisdom" of the campus fountain. The quad was mostly empty, the late afternoon sun casting long shadows. I sat down beside her on the bench, the silence stretching for a moment, filled only by the splash of recycled water and the distant city hum.

"Hey," I said softly.

She glanced up, one eyebrow raised in that way that meant *What now?* but didn't reply, just went back to shading the grotesque caricature of a politician she was drawing.

"About the competition," I started, then hesitated. "Look, I get it. I really do. It feels wrong. It probably *is* wrong. Sterling's slime is all over it."

She kept drawing, but I saw her knuckles tighten on the pen.

"But," I continued, choosing my words carefully, "what if... what if *we* just went to the first audition? Not necessarily to enter the whole band right away. Just to see. To scope it out. See who else shows up, see how they run things. Reconnaissance." I tried a small smile. "Think of it like... casing the joint. Just you and me, Gem. Like old times?" I was laying it on a bit thick, maybe, but I knew appealing to our friendship, our history, was the best way to get her to consider something she was dead set against.

She stopped drawing, looked out at the quad, her expression unreadable.

"Why, Jess?" she asked quietly, finally meeting my eyes. "Why do you want this so bad?"

The question hung there. *Because I want us to be more than this? Because I want my parents off my back? Because I'm scared of ending up playing dive bars forever? Because part of me craves the validation, even if it's tainted? Because I want... something more with you, and maybe this is a fucked-up way to try and make a space for that?* I couldn't say any of that.

"I don't know," I admitted, looking down at my hands. "Maybe... maybe I just want to see if we *can*. If we're good enough. And maybe..." I took a breath, trying a different angle, one that felt closer to a truth I could actually speak. "Maybe it would be... interesting? To just go check it out? See what the machine looks like from the inside? You're always sketching things, observing... think of it as field research." I risked a glance at her. Maybe framing it as information gathering, something closer to her own way of processing the world, would work. And maybe, just maybe, the idea of doing it together, facing this weird corporate beast side-by-side, appealed to her too, even if she wouldn't admit it.

Gemini studied my face for a long moment, her gaze sharp, analytical. I felt pinned, exposed, like she could see every calculation, every mixed motive. Then, slowly, infuriatingly, a tiny, almost imperceptible smile touched the corner of her mouth. She sighed, a long, drawn-out sound that seemed to carry the weight of the whole damn city.

"Fine," she said, turning back to her sketchbook. "Reconnaissance. *We* check out the auditions. Together." Her emphasis on 'we' felt deliberate, acknowledging the unspoken implication – this wasn't just about me, it was about the band, even if I'd framed it personally. "But Jess?" She paused, her pen hovering over the page. "If it feels like the cage door is closing, even a crack, we bolt. No arguments. Deal?"

Relief washed over me, quickly followed by a fresh wave of anxiety. "Deal," I said, maybe a little too quickly.

We sat in silence for another minute, the fountain splashing, the city humming its low, dissonant song. We were going to check out Freedom's Ring. Stepping onto thin ice didn't even begin to cover it.

CHAPTER 4: GEMINI

The address for the "Freedom's Ring" preliminary auditions wasn't some dingy warehouse or repurposed community center tucked away on a forgotten side street. Of course not. This was Sterling territory. The venue was the Sterling Grand Auditorium, a gleaming, vaguely menacing monument to corporate self-aggrandizement smack in the heart of downtown GLAMA. All sharp angles, reflective smoked glass that probably hid surveillance systems, and imposing steel beams designed to convey power and permanence. The kind of place that usually hosted black-tie symphony galas, slick touring Broadway musicals about sanitized historical figures, or, most fittingly, Sterling Corp shareholder meetings where profits were celebrated and dissent was quietly escorted out by security. Pulling up in Jessica's parents' plush, silent minivan felt less like arriving for a band audition and more like attempting to infiltrate the Death Star in a slightly used family vehicle. Which, I suppose, was exactly what we were doing. Reconnaissance. Right.

"Subtle," I muttered, leaning forward from the back seat to take in the enormous "Freedom's Ring" banner draped across the imposing facade. It featured Sterling's airbrushed, eerily benevolent smiling face superimposed over a stylized, hyper-clean GLAMA skyline, complete with a fluttering, digitally rendered flag graphic. The tagline screamed: "GLAMA's Heart Beats Strong!" Tasteful. Understated. Utterly nauseating. My blue mohawk probably stood out like a sore thumb against all this corporate polish.

"It's... professional," Rhys offered from beside me, already craning his neck, eyes wide with something dangerously close to awe as he took in the scale of the building, the uniformed valets (valets! for an audition!), the general aura of expensive importance. "Serious setup."

"It's branded," Leo corrected quietly from the other side, his gaze sharp, analytical, scanning the entrance. "Every inch of it." He was right. Even the damn revolving doors had tiny, etched Sterling logos on the glass. Security guards in crisp, vaguely militaristic grey uniforms – Sterling Security, naturally, the ubiquitous private force that seemed to be replacing actual GLAMA PD in wealthier districts – stood flanking the polished glass doors, checking IDs against lists on handheld Sterling™ tablets with practiced, impersonal efficiency.

"Alright, Operation Trojan Horse," Jessica said from the driver's seat, trying for a light, breezy tone that didn't quite mask the tension in her shoulders as she navigated the minivan into the designated loading zone. It wasn't a grimy alley but a surprisingly clean and brightly lit underground bay, complete with numbered parking spots and piped-in instrumental music that sounded suspiciously like a Sterling Media easy-listening station. A stark contrast to The Rat Hole's dumpster-adjacent ambiance. "Remember the plan," she continued, cutting the engine. "We go in, play one song for the initial screening, check the vibe, see who else crawled out from under a rock for this thing, and then we make a decision. No commitments yet." She glanced at me in the rearview mirror, her eyes meeting mine for a fraction of a second. "And Gem? Try not to look like you're actively plotting arson or composing revolutionary manifestos in your head."

"No promises," I grumbled, wrestling my heavy bass amp out of the van's luxurious cargo space. "This place practically begs for a manifesto. Or at least some strategically placed graffiti."

The holding area backstage – or rather, *pre*-stage, since this was just the initial cattle call designed to weed out the obviously untalented or insufficiently compliant – was a vast, soul-crushingly beige conference room. It smelled faintly of industrial carpet cleaner trying, and failing, to mask the underlying scent of nervous sweat and cheap hairspray.

Fluorescent lights hummed aggressively overhead, casting a sterile, unflattering glare on the dozens of other musicians milling about, clutching instruments and forced smiles. It was a jarringly eclectic, almost surreal mix. Slick pop hopefuls with impossibly perfect hair and meticulously coordinated outfits practiced synchronized dance moves and vocal warm-ups in corners, their faces masks of determined ambition. Intense-looking metal dudes dressed head-to-toe in black leather compared elaborate, multi-pedaled guitar rigs, muttering about tone and gain stages. Earnest folk singers with acoustic guitars strapped to their backs looked wide-eyed and lost, like sheep accidentally wandered into a wolf convention. And then there were the punks – a smaller contingent, recognizable by their ripped band shirts, safety pins, and varying degrees of brightly dyed hair.

I even spotted the guys from Asphalt Vomit, a thrash band we'd played a disastrous double bill with at The Rat Hole last year; their guitarist, a dude who went by 'Maggot,' was trying to look nonchalant while clutching a guitar case covered in anarchist stickers that seemed to scream in protest against the beige walls. They, like the rest of us who'd crawled out from under GLAMA's grittier rocks, looked distinctly uncomfortable under the fluorescent glare, eyeing the corporate surroundings and the pop acts with varying degrees of suspicion, amusement, or outright hostility. A tribe displaced.

I immediately flipped open my sketchbook, needing to process the sheer cognitive dissonance of it all, the weird collision of underground culture and corporate branding. My pen found the page, translating the scene into sharp, angular lines. The synth-pop duo, male and female, identical platinum blonde bobs and matching silver jumpsuits that looked like rejects from a low-budget sci-fi movie, practiced pouting poses in front of a mirrored column. *Synthēsis,* the sign-in sheet had called them. Perfect name. All glossy surface, zero detectable substance. Nearby, a quartet of guys who looked like they'd time-traveled directly from a 1970s prog-rock documentary – complete with beards, bell-bottoms, and expressions of profound concentration – meticulously tuned complex-looking instruments, including a double-necked guitar and something that looked suspiciously like a keytar. *Axiom Quartet.* No singer in sight. All complex time signatures and emotionless technical proficiency. Safe. Sterile. Approved.

And then I saw them. Holding court near the complimentary Sterling™ Brand Purified Water dispenser, naturally. Iron Eagle. Four guys radiating smug entitlement like cheap cologne. They were dressed in expensive-looking black leather jackets – not worn-in thrift store finds, but designer approximations of punk gear – adorned with subtle but unmistakable nationalist patches: stylized eagles clutching bundles of arrows, vaguely runic symbols that prickled the back of my neck, maybe even a discreetly placed GLAMA flag. Their gear, stacked neatly beside them on professional road cases, looked brand new, top-of-the-line –

Marshalls, Gibsons, stuff that cost more than my entire student loan debt for the year. Way beyond what most gigging punk bands could afford unless they had serious backing. Sterling's backing? Seemed likely. Unlike the rest of us who looked like we'd accidentally stumbled into a corporate retreat, Iron Eagle lounged with an air of ownership, as if the Sterling™ Brand Purified Water was drawn from their private well. They weren't talking to anyone else, just laughing too loudly amongst themselves, projecting an aura of bored, aggressive superiority that felt perfectly at home amidst the brushed steel and hushed reverence of the auditorium. Their frontman, Kane Krieger, a guy with close-cropped, bleached hair, sharp features, and eyes as cold and empty as chipped ice, caught my stare from across the room. He didn't look away. Instead, he gave me a slow, deliberate smirk, a look of such blatant dismissal and implied threat that it felt like a physical blow. *You don't belong here.* My own fierce features probably mirrored some of that back at him; my eyebrows arched automatically.

"There they are," Leo murmured beside me, his voice tight, his usual buoyant energy completely extinguished. "Sterling's pet fascists. Didn't take long."

Rhys, who'd been openly admiring Iron Eagle's gleaming Marshall stack from afar, frowned, his brow furrowing in confusion. "Come on, Leo, they're just another band. Maybe a little intense, but..." He glanced towards Jessica. "Probably just got a rich dad backing them, like Jess." He elbowed Jessica playfully, completely missing the venom in Leo's tone and the sudden stiffness in Jessica's posture.

Jessica flinched slightly at the comparison but didn't reply, her attention fixed on Iron Eagle, a worried crease deepening between her brows. She saw it too, maybe not the ideology yet, but the arrogance, the implied connection to power.

"They're not *just* another band, Rhys," I said, keeping my voice low but sharp. "Pay attention to the patches. Look at the symbols. Listen to their lyrics sometime, if you can stomach lines about 'purifying the homeland.' Especially from Krieger."

"Whatever," Rhys mumbled, turning back to fiddle with his own guitar tuner, clearly uncomfortable with the confrontation, retreating into the safe zone of gear talk. "They sound tight on their recordings, though. Really professional." Professional. Like the security guards. Like the judges. Like Sterling himself.

Before I could retort that fascism often *did* sound tight and professional, at least initially, a woman with a laminated badge clipped to her Sterling Corp polo shirt called out our name, her voice echoing slightly in the cavernous room. "Jessica's Jones? You're up next. Stage B." Her smile was wide, bright, professionally applied, and utterly devoid of warmth.

We followed her through a maze of identical beige, carpeted hallways – the kind designed to disorient and pacify – to a smaller performance space off the main auditorium. Still, it was bigger and cleaner than any stage we'd ever played before. It had professional track lighting bathing the small stage in a sterile white glow, multiple cameras bearing the SNN logo positioned strategically on tripods, and a long table draped in black cloth where three judges sat looking profoundly bored, scrolling through tablets. Sterling branding was everywhere – subtle logos on the mic stands, a large "Freedom's Ring" banner serving as the backdrop, even embossed on the damn disposable water bottles sitting untouched on the judges' table. It felt less like an audition and more like stepping onto the set of a corporate training video about synergy and brand alignment.

"One song," the polo-shirt woman chirped, gesturing towards the stage with a clipboard. "Give it your best! Make GLAMA proud!" She delivered the line with the forced enthusiasm of someone contractually obligated to believe the hype.

We plugged in quickly, the silence in the room feeling heavy, awkward, amplified by the professional setting. The usual pre-gig buzz of nervous energy felt dampened, replaced by a kind of wary tension. "Free to Be?" Jessica whispered, looking at me for confirmation, her eyes wide.

I nodded. It was the obvious choice for the *screening* – catchy enough to potentially pass muster, but with lyrics that felt like a small, necessary act of defiance just singing them aloud in this sterilized, corporate space. A tiny crack in their smooth facade.

Mack counted us in, her sticks clicking with sharp precision, and we launched into it. Playing here felt... weird. Wrong. The sound was too clean, too controlled, bouncing strangely off the acoustically treated walls. The room seemed to absorb the energy rather than reflecting it back like the sweaty confines of The Rat Hole did. There was no chaotic, pulsing crowd to feed off, just the three judges occasionally making notes on their tablets with stylus pens and the impassive, dark lenses of the SNN cameras staring back at us like judgmental eyes.

Leo's trumpet, usually so bright and soaring, sounded almost lonely without the usual swirling chaos to lift it. Rhys played competently, hitting all the notes, but seemed slightly intimidated by the setting, his usual stage presence shrinking under the lights. Jessica's playing was technically perfect, each note precise, each chord change flawless, but it lacked the fire, the raw edge I'd heard in the garage just nights before. She kept her eyes closed for most of the song, as if retreating inward, away from the judges' scrutiny.

Only Mack seemed unfazed, utterly impervious to the environment. She laid down her solid, grounding beat with the same focused intensity she always had, whether playing to fifty slam-dancing punks or three bored judges and a camera crew. Her drumming was the anchor holding the rest of us together.

I stepped up to the shared mic, trying to inject the feeling, the yearning, the coded meaning into the lyrics, but the words seemed to get lost in the sterile acoustics, swallowed by the professional silence. "Who you are behind the mask / Is that too much for us to ask?" The question felt particularly pointed here, in this temple of manufactured image and corporate-approved authenticity.

I saw one of the judges, a man with slicked-back grey hair and an expensive, tailored suit that probably cost more than my semester's tuition, raise a single, perfectly sculpted eyebrow. He tapped something into his tablet with a decisive flick of his wrist. The other two judges – a woman with severe glasses and a tight bun, and a younger guy trying too hard to look cool in a leather jacket over a Sterling Music Group t-shirt – remained impassive.

We finished the song. The silence that followed was absolute, heavy, broken only by the incessant hum of the fluorescent lights. It stretched for an uncomfortable beat.

"Thank you," said the judge who'd raised his eyebrow, his voice smooth, modulated, utterly noncommittal. Like a voice synthesized by an AI trained on executive board meetings. "Impressive energy." He glanced down at his tablet. "Technically proficient." Another glance. "A little... raw, perhaps, for the 'Freedom's Ring' brand identity, but interesting potential." He offered a brief, dismissive nod. "We'll be in touch via the portal regarding advancement to the preliminary rounds." It felt less like an evaluation and more like a polite brush-off wrapped in layers of corporate jargon. We were dismissed.

"What the hell was that?" Leo hissed as soon as we were back in the beige holding area, shoving his trumpet angrily back into its case. "Did you see their faces? They barely listened! They were probably checking their SterlingCoin™ portfolios!"

"They listened," I said quietly, carefully wiping down the strings of my bass, the familiar ritual calming my own jangled nerves. "They just didn't *hear*. Or maybe they heard exactly what they wanted to hear – potential product they think they can shape. Sand off the edges, auto-tune the vocals, add a synth line, slap a Sterling logo on it."

"But he said we had potential!" Rhys insisted, his earlier awe now curdled into anxious hope. He clutched his guitar case like a life raft. "He said 'impressive energy'! That's good, right? That means they liked us!"

"It's corporate speak, Rhys," I sighed, feeling suddenly exhausted. "It means 'You're loud and maybe marketable if you tone down the politics, ditch the reggae, and don't say anything inconvenient.' It means 'maybe,' which usually means 'no,' unless they think they can exploit us."

Just then, Iron Eagle swaggered past us, looking like they'd just come from Stage A, radiating smug confidence. Their frontman, Kane, deliberately bumped Leo's shoulder, the first time one of *them* had initiated physical contact, almost knocking the trumpet case from his hand. He looked us up and down, his lip curling in a sneer. "You're not even punk," he spat, his voice dripping with contempt, his eyes lingering on me for an extra beat. "Just low-rent island import trash."

The air went still. The insult, ugly and specific, hung there, targeting not just our music but *me*, my identity, the reggae roots grounding our sound. Leo clenched his fists, stepping forward, his face flushing dark with anger. "You want to say that again, you fascist piece of–"

Mack moved then, not aggressively, but with a swift, economical motion that put her solid frame directly between Leo and Krieger. Her hand didn't grab Leo's arm, but rested firmly on his chest, a physical stop sign. "Leo," she said, her voice low, calm, but carrying an unmistakable weight of command learned in places none of us wanted to imagine. "Stand down. Tactical retreat."

Kane laughed, a harsh, ugly sound that echoed slightly in the big room. "Listen to your mommy, horn boy." He gave Mack a long, deliberately intimidating look, trying to stare her down. Mack didn't flinch, didn't react at all, just met his gaze with that unnerving, absolute calm until *he* looked away first, a flicker of uncertainty, maybe even fear, crossing his face before he masked it with another sneer. "Whatever," he spat. "Enjoy obscurity." He jerked his head at his bandmates, and they swaggered off towards the exit, laughing amongst themselves.

The tense silence they left behind crackled. Leo finally let out a shaky breath, rubbing his shoulder where the guy had hit him. "Horn boy, huh?" he muttered, trying for humor but his voice still tight with anger. "Is that just a Nazi thing now, or what?"

Something inside me snapped. Ignited. The condescension, the casual fascism, the racist, classist dismissal disguised as musical gatekeeping, the smug certainty that they *owned* this space, this city, this *sound* ... it was too much. Seeing them walk away like that, knowing they represented everything Sterling wanted this competition to be, knowing they'd probably sail through to the next round on a wave of corporate approval and ideological alignment... No. We couldn't just walk away. We couldn't let *them* be the only voice representing punk, representing anger, representing *anything* real in this polished, sterile, corporate farce. My earlier cynicism felt like a luxury I couldn't afford anymore. It felt like surrender.

"We're doing it," I said, the words tasting like metal and adrenaline in my mouth. My own voice sounded hard, unfamiliar.

Everyone looked at me, surprised. Even Mack raised an eyebrow slightly.

"We're entering," I clarified, looking straight at Jessica first, then letting my gaze sweep over Leo and Rhys. "Screw the reconnaissance. Screw the cage. If those assholes are in, then *we* need to be in. We can't just cede this ground to them, let them define what punk is in this city, let them win before the fight even starts." I gripped the neck of my bass tighter. "We have to show people what real music sounds like, what real anger feels like. Even if they cut the cameras, even if the judges hate us, even if we crash and burn. We have to try." The words tumbled out, fueled by a sudden, unexpected surge of pure, righteous fury, amplified by Krieger's ugly words.

Rhys's face lit up like a Sterling™ brand holiday display. "Yes! I knew you'd see it! This is gonna be huge!"

Leo nodded slowly, a determined glint replacing the frustration in his eyes. He looked at me, a silent question about my sudden reversal, but then determination firmed his jaw. "Okay. Yeah. Okay. Let's do it. Let's show them what Jessica's Jones is really about."

Jessica looked torn, biting her lip again, glancing nervously from me back towards the exit where Iron Eagle had disappeared, then finally back at me. "Are you sure, Gem?" she asked hesitantly, her voice barely a whisper. "You said... about the cage?"

I met her eyes, holding her gaze. I saw the fear there, but also a flicker of something else – maybe relief that I wasn't just shutting it down, maybe even a spark of shared defiance. "I know what I said," I replied, keeping my voice steady despite the tremor I felt inside. "And the deal still stands." I looked around at the others, making sure they heard. "The second it feels like we're losing ourselves, the second they try to muzzle us too hard, the second it stops being *our* fight and starts being *their* show, we bolt. No arguments. Deal?"

Rhys and Leo nodded eagerly. Jessica hesitated for another fraction of a second, then gave a small, tight nod. "Deal," she agreed, the word barely audible.

We found the polo-shirt woman near the exit, her smile firmly, professionally in place. We filled out the official entry forms on a sleek Sterling™ tablet, scrolling past pages of dense legal text we didn't read, signing away our digital souls in triplicate with a stylus that felt unnervingly like a weapon. We were assigned a slot for the first judged preliminary round later that week. It felt less like entering a competition and more like signing a pact with the devil, using his own branded pen.

The first official preliminary round felt different. More real, somehow more dangerous than the initial screening. We were back at the Sterling Grand Auditorium, ushered this time into a slightly larger, more formal theater space. The lights felt brighter, hotter. More SNN cameras glided silently on robotic arms, their red recording lights glowing like malevolent eyes. The audience was bigger too, though still sparsely populated – a scattering of nervous parents clutching laminated programs, bored-looking industry scouts in expensive jackets conspicuously checking their phones, and a phalanx of Sterling Corp junior executives in identical dark suits occupying the front rows, their faces impassive masks of corporate loyalty. The air conditioning hummed loudly, keeping the room unnaturally cold, sucking the energy out before it could even build.

We were scheduled to play "Torn to Shreds." It felt like the right choice after the Iron Eagle encounter – angry, critical of the system, but maybe not quite provocative enough to get us instantly disqualified. It was a statement, but perhaps one the judges could still dismiss as generic punk angst if they chose to. A calculated risk. Still, stepping onto this stage felt like a betrayal of everything we stood for, even playing this song. Backstage – another beige room, this one with slightly less desperate-smelling carpet – felt even more tense than before. Bands huddled in nervous clusters, practicing harmonies in hushed tones, avoiding eye contact. The easy camaraderie of the dive bar scene, the shared sense of being outsiders together, felt a million miles away. This was competition, raw and undisguised, pitting artist against artist for the corporate machine's approval.

Iron Eagle played just before us. They strode onto the stage with arrogant confidence, launching into a technically proficient but soulless blast of Oi!-inflected punk rock, all power chords and shouted slogans about strength and purity. Their sound was huge, almost unnaturally loud and polished – no doubt the work of that mountain of top-dollar gear they somehow possessed. Maybe Rhys was right about rich parents, or maybe, as I suspected, Sterling's media arm provided more than just favorable coverage. The lyrics were barely veiled nationalist garbage, but the small contingent of their fans near the front ate it up, shouting along, throwing fists in the air. The judges nodded along, tapping notes onto their tablets. The Sterling execs watched with faint smiles. It was exactly the kind of controlled, pseudo-rebellious noise the regime could tolerate, even encourage. They finished to thunderous applause from their section and polite, slightly bewildered clapping from the rest of the room.

Then it was our turn. Walking onto that brightly lit stage felt like stepping into an interrogation room. The silence from the audience pressed down, vast and judgmental. Mack counted us in, her rhythm solid as ever, and we launched into "Torn to Shreds." I tried to channel the anger from the holding room, the disgust at Iron Eagle, the feeling of being trapped in this corporate machine, into my playing. I dug deep into the strings, pushing the reggae groove under the punk fury, wanting the lyrics about the system chewing people up to hit hard. The song felt tight, focused, maybe *too* focused. I felt hyper-aware of the cameras sweeping across us, the judges' impassive faces below, the weight of expectation. The cold room seemed to swallow the sound, deadening the raw energy we usually thrived on.

I glanced over at my bandmates. Rhys played with fierce concentration, his brow furrowed, desperate to impress, occasionally risking a quick, anxious glance towards the judges. Leo's trumpet blasts cut through the mix, sharp and defiant, but his usual stage presence felt constrained, less joyful bouncing, more coiled tension. Jessica shredded her solo flawlessly, a cascade of perfectly executed notes, a display of pure technical skill, but she kept her eyes squeezed shut almost the entire time, lost somewhere behind her eyelids, maybe retreating from the sterile environment, maybe just focusing intensely to avoid any mistakes. Even Mack's drumming, while precise and powerful, seemed to have an extra edge of controlled violence tonight, each beat landing like a perfectly placed blow against an invisible enemy. We were playing *well*, maybe the tightest we'd ever played, but something felt missing. The connection. The fire. The feeling of *us* against *them*. Here, it felt like *us* under *their* microscope.

We finished the song. The applause afterward was polite, scattered, maybe slightly confused. We weren't slick and polished like Synthēsis, who had performed earlier with flawless choreography and auto-tuned vocals that sounded like they were generated by an algorithm. We weren't technically dazzling and safely instrumental like Axiom Quartet, who had impressed the judges with their complex musicianship but said absolutely nothing. And we definitely weren't spewing the aggressive, nationalist bile Iron Eagle had delivered. We didn't quite fit into any of the approved boxes. We were just... loud. And maybe, hopefully, a little bit dangerous, even if the room didn't seem to know what to do with it.

As we were clearing our gear off the stage, weaving through cables and stagehands in matching Sterling™ crew shirts who moved with brisk, impersonal efficiency, I saw him approach Jessica. A man in an expensive, sharply tailored charcoal suit, moving with the easy confidence of someone who owned every room he walked into. He had smooth, ageless features – the kind achieved through expensive skincare and maybe minor cosmetic procedures – professionally whitened teeth that gleamed unnaturally under the stage lights, and eyes that didn't quite smile when his mouth did. He looked like every blandly handsome news anchor or corporate spokesperson on SNN. He intercepted Jessica before she reached the wings, extending a perfectly manicured hand.

I lingered nearby, pretending to adjust a knob on my amp, close enough to catch the drift over the crew chatter and the next band sound-checking.

"Jessica Lamas, right?" His voice was smooth as silk, cultured, the kind of voice used to selling luxury products or political lies with equal ease. Jessica looked startled, nodding hesitantly as she shook his hand. "Rick Anderson, Executive Producer, Sterling Entertainment Division. Just wanted to say – fantastic energy up there. Really... raw." He delivered the word 'raw' like it was something interesting but potentially unsanitary, something that needed processing.

"Oh. Uh, thanks," Jessica stammered, clearly flustered by the unexpected attention from someone with such an important-sounding title. I saw her unconsciously smooth down her shirt.

"You kids have real talent," Anderson continued, leaning in slightly, lowering his voice conspiratorially, creating a bubble of false intimacy in the backstage bustle. "Big things could happen. Important people are watching this competition, you know? People who appreciate... harmony." He paused, letting the word hang in the air, freighted with unspoken meaning. "On stage and off." His eyes flickered briefly towards Jessica's expensive cherry-red Les Paul – a clear sign he knew exactly who she was – then back to her face. "I know your father slightly – David Lamas, the dentist, right? Important man. Does great work for the community."

He dropped the name casually, like mentioning a mutual acquaintance at a country club, but the effect was immediate. From my vantage point, I saw Jessica go pale, her posture stiffening almost imperceptibly. *We know who you are. We know who your family is.* The message, cloaked in polite professional networking, was unmistakable. "It's a sensitive time in GLAMA," Anderson went on, his smile never wavering, radiating professional sincerity. "Wouldn't want any... unnecessary static... to cause problems for anyone." He glanced around the backstage area, as if sharing a profound secret. "Families appreciate stability, right? It's all about finding the right message." He patted her shoulder lightly, a gesture that looked friendly but felt possessive, proprietary, like branding cattle. "Just keep that positive energy flowing, keep the message upbeat and unifying. That's what connects with audiences. That's the 'Freedom's Ring' spirit." He gave her another blindingly white, perfectly calibrated smile. "Looking forward to seeing more from

Jessica's Jones."

And then he was gone, melting back into the backstage bustle as smoothly and silently as he had appeared. Jessica stood frozen for a moment, rooted to the spot, her hand still half-raised from the handshake. Her eyes were wide, staring after him, the color drained from her face. I didn't need to hear her thoughts to know what that felt like – the sudden, chilling realization that the abstract dangers we talked about, the ones she could usually ignore thanks to her family's status, had just become terrifyingly concrete. The safety net she usually took for granted, the one woven from her parents' wealth and connections, suddenly felt like a leash, held firmly by Sterling's perfectly manicured, invisible hand.

The cage door hadn't slammed shut yet, not quite. But I could definitely hear the hinges starting to creak, loud and clear. And I knew, watching the fear bloom in Jessica's eyes, that things had just gotten a whole lot more complicated.

CHAPTER 5:
RHYS KELLY

Okay, maybe Gemini was right about the judges being corporate suits looking for malleable product, and maybe Leo was right about Iron Eagle being grade-A assholes (Krieger definitely was, trying to stare down Mack like that? Seriously?), but they couldn't deny the one crucial fact: we made it through. Jessica's Jones was officially advancing in the Freedom's Ring competition. We were in.

Walking across the GLAMA U campus the following Monday felt... different. It wasn't like a spotlight suddenly followed me or anything, no crowds parted, but *I* felt different. Less like just another face shuffling between classes, more like someone with potential, someone on the verge. We weren't just jamming in Jessica's garage anymore; we'd played on that professional stage, under those bright lights, in front of those SNN cameras. We got the email confirmation over the weekend – a slick, Sterling-branded notification congratulating us on advancing to the Quarterfinals. *Quarterfinals!* I'd screenshotted it immediately, cropping out the generic text and just leaving the logo and our band name, then sent it straight to my Dad.

His reply was almost instant, buzzing my phone during Econ 101: *Fantastic news, Rhys! Knew you had it in you. Keep focused! This could be the start of something.* Even Mom, who usually just asked if band practice interfered with my studying (or reminded me that my older brother, Mark, had just closed another big deal at his Sterling-affiliated law firm, or that my sister, Chloe, was captaining her university soccer team to another championship), texted back: *That's nice, dear. Don't forget your Political Science midterm is next week.* Okay, so maybe not total enthusiasm from her, but Dad sounded genuinely proud. That felt good. Really good. It wasn't like with Mark, whose achievements always seemed to echo louder, or Chloe, whose athletic trophies filled the shelves. They were the stars. I was... well, I played guitar. Dad always said, "Find your passion, Rhys, that's what matters," but I knew he worried I wasn't as driven as my siblings, that I was still drifting. Maybe this competition was my way to finally show them, to earn that specific kind of validation, the kind that felt solid, real.

I actually found myself humming the main riff from "Torn to Shreds" walking past the Fountain of Wisdom, picturing it blasting out over a huge festival crowd, picturing myself nailing the rhythm part perfectly, maybe even getting a quick close-up shot. The song *had* felt good on that stage, objectively. Tight, powerful. Sure, Gemini got weird about the "feel" sometimes, always wanting more 'space' or some vague 'political edge', but technically, we nailed it. My Strat sounded absolutely killer through their massive sound system, way better than through my practice amp. That stage manager, the one with the clipboard? She even complimented my playing afterward, a quick "Killer guitar work!" as we cleared off. *Killer.* That wasn't corporate speak; that was real.

Over the next week or so, the competition itself started to blow up, just like Dad predicted. You couldn't avoid it. SNN ran nightly highlight packages – slickly edited montages set to driving, vaguely patriotic rock anthems, full of quick cuts, dramatic lighting, and slow-motion shots of musicians looking passionate. They mostly featured the really polished acts, the ones who looked like they were already stars. That synth-pop duo Synthēsis was everywhere, their catchy, meaningless hooks burrowing into your brain. Apparently, they had a huge online following already, all pastel aesthetics and synchronized dance moves. Then there was that folk group, Heartwood, all wholesome harmonies and acoustic guitars, singing earnest songs about "GLAMA heritage" and "community spirit" that sounded suspiciously like rewritten national anthems. Feel-good, safe stuff. The kind of thing Sterling himself probably listened to.

Iron Eagle got a *ton* of screen time too. Lots of aggressive posturing, shots of their frontman, Kane, sneering into the camera or power-posing with his expensive-looking guitar, all cut together with quick bursts of their loudest, simplest riffs. They looked like rock stars, the dangerous kind, but maybe dangerous in a way the producers liked? SNN commentators praised their "uncompromising energy," their "raw power," and their "passionate defense of traditional GLAMA values." Gemini would probably call it pure propaganda, framing fascists as patriots. Maybe it was, a little, but you couldn't deny it was effective. People online were talking about them constantly, arguing about them in comment sections, sharing their clips. They had buzz. Major buzz.

Jessica's Jones? We got maybe three seconds total in one montage later in the week – a quick, slightly blurry shot of Jessica playing her solo from "Torn to Shreds," eyes closed, hair falling across her face, looking intense. No mention of the band name, no context. If you blinked, you missed it. Typical. Probably Gemini's fault for writing lyrics that were too "raw," like that judge said. Too negative. Or maybe it was Leo's trumpet? Ska wasn't exactly mainstream arena rock. Still, we were *in*. We had advanced. That was the important thing. We just needed a better strategy for the next round.

"Dude, did you see the Freedom's Ring forums?" I asked Leo later that week as we slumped into seats near the back of the cavernous lecture hall for 'History of Rock and Roll'. Professor Davies hadn't arrived yet, but the low murmur of pre-class chatter filled the air. Davies was cool, kind of an old hippie burnout who mostly just played scratchy old vinyl records and told rambling stories about seeing legendary bands back in the day. Easy A, but Leo always seemed bored out of his mind, preferring to scroll through depressing news feeds on his tablet. "People are going nuts on there," I continued, pulling up the forum on my phone. "Already picking favorites for the finals. Synthēsis is huge, obviously. And Iron Eagle... man, people either love 'em or hate 'em, but they're talking." I even saw some comments praising their "strong stance" on "keeping GLAMA values pure," which sounded a bit like what those SNN commentators were saying. Some other threads were getting pretty heated about that new "Family Harmony Act" too – a lot of angry stuff, but also a surprising number of people saying it was about time someone "defended traditional families." It was confusing, all the noise.

Leo just grunted, still focused on his tablet – probably casualty figures from some border skirmish or another depressing political analysis he felt obligated to consume. "Don't read that garbage, Rhys. It's all manufactured hype. Astroturfed comments, probably paid for by Sterling himself to stir up controversy and make his pet fascists seem relevant."

"How do you *know*?" I challenged, slightly annoyed by his instant dismissal. It felt like he and Gemini just automatically hated anything popular or successful. "Maybe people just like them? They're tight. They have energy. And some of those comments about the Harmony Act... I mean, SNN said it's just about protecting families, right? Keeping things stable. That doesn't sound so bad."

Leo finally looked up, his eyes narrowed. "Protecting *which* families, Rhys? And stable for *whom*?"

"It's just music, man," I sighed, leaning back in the uncomfortable plastic seat, not wanting to get into another heavy political debate. Why did they always have to make everything so negative? Couldn't we just enjoy the fact that we were in a major competition with a real shot at something big? Why dissect everything until all the fun was gone?

Professor Davies shuffled in then, tweed jacket slightly rumpled, glasses perched on the end of his nose. He dropped a stack of vinyl onto the lectern, adjusted the microphone with a squeal of feedback, and peered out at us. "Alright, settle down, future rock historians, or future accountants who needed an easy arts credit." A few dutiful chuckles. "Today, we backtrack. Before Elvis, before Chuck Berry, before the electric guitar even really learned how to scream, there was folk. Music of the people. Music with a message."

Oh great. Politics again. I slumped lower in my seat, pulling out my phone to check the gear forums.

Davies put a record on the turntable connected to the lecture hall's surprisingly decent sound system. A scratchy voice, accompanied by a simple acoustic guitar, filled the room. It wasn't rock and roll, not even close. It was plain, kinda twangy, telling some story about dust storms and migrants. I recognized the name when Davies mentioned it – Woody Guthrie. Some old folk singer Gemini had on a couple of worn-out t-shirts.

"Now, Woody wasn't just singing about lost love or pickup trucks," Davies said, pacing slowly in front of the projection screen, which now showed a black and white photo of a serious-looking guy with a guitar. "He was singing about injustice. About poverty. About workers' rights. About fascists." He paused for emphasis. "He saw music as a tool. A weapon, even."

My attention snagged on that word. *Weapon.* It sounded like something Gemini would say.

Davies continued, "He famously had a slogan painted right on his guitar." He clicked a button, and another image appeared on the screen: a close-up of Guthrie's acoustic guitar, simple block letters scrawled across it. "THIS MACHINE KILLS FASCISTS."

My breath caught. That was it. The sticker. The faded, peeling sticker Gemini slapped on every bass she owned, the one she smoothed down like a ritual before every practice. *That's* where it came from. Some old folk singer.

Suddenly, Gemini's obsession with that sticker made a different kind of sense. It wasn't just random punk aggression; it was... historical. Connected to something. She was always doing that – making these obscure references, seeing connections nobody else did. It was annoying as hell sometimes, how she acted like she was smarter than everyone else, how she dismissed things *I* thought were cool, like Iron Eagle's sound or getting ahead in the competition. How she spent more time meticulously cleaning her bass and positioning that damn sticker than she ever spent just... hanging out.

I pictured her now, probably back at her apartment, hunched over that bass, mohawk slicked back, fingers tracing the worn wood, maybe humming some weird reggae bassline only she could hear. Sometimes, when Leo was playing a trumpet line, I'd try to mimic it on my guitar, just for fun, trying to catch the vibe. Gemini would just give me that look, that one-eyebrow-raised thing, like I was missing the point. She treated that instrument with more care and attention than she treated most people, including me. There was this intensity about her, this focused passion, whether it was her music or her politics or her stupid sticker. It was infuriating. It was also... kind of amazing. If she could just channel that energy into something *productive*, like winning this competition, instead of fighting lost causes...

If she ever looked at *me* with half the intensity she looked at that sticker, or her bass... The thought surfaced unexpectedly, making my face feel hot. I pushed it away immediately. Ridiculous. She barely tolerated me most of the time. Still. That phrase... *This Machine Kills Fascists.* It sounded powerful. Maybe there was something to it after all. Even if it came from some dusty old folk song instead of a killer guitar solo.

As the lecture ended and students started gathering their things, the Guthrie image still lingering on the screen, I nudged Leo. "Hey, check that out," I said, pointing to the projected photo of the guitar. "That sticker Gemini has? It's from this guy. Woody Guthrie."

Leo glanced at the screen, then back at me, a flicker of surprise followed by something like weary patience in his eyes. "Yeah, Rhys. I know. Woody Guthrie. Folk singer. Union organizer. Anti-fascist."

"Right," I said, feeling slightly defensive. "So... I guess Gemini's into folk music then? Didn't really seem like her style." I pictured her listening to twangy acoustic guitars and harmonica solos. It didn't compute.

Leo sighed softly, shaking his head as he packed his tablet away. "Rhys, man, it's not about the *genre*. It's not about whether it's folk or punk or ska or whatever noise we make." He zipped his bag shut and looked at me directly, his usual bright energy replaced by a quiet seriousness that made me uncomfortable. "It's about the *why*. Why did Guthrie write that on his guitar? Why does Gemini put it on her bass?"

I shrugged, feeling put on the spot. "To look tough? To be political?"

"Maybe," Leo conceded, "but it's more than that. Guthrie sang about people who were hurting, people who were ignored, people getting screwed over by the system – by banks, by bosses, by politicians, by fascists. He sang *for* them. He tried to make other people *feel* what they were feeling." He paused, letting the words sink in, his gaze searching mine. "It's about empathy, Rhys. Seeing someone else's struggle and making it yours, even for just the length of a song. Making people *care*. That's the machine that kills fascists. Not the guitar itself, but the connection it makes, the feeling." He slung his bag over his shoulder. "Gemini gets that. That's why the sticker matters to her. It's not just about being angry; it's about *who* you're angry for."

He didn't wait for a reply, just headed out into the crowded hallway, leaving me sitting there feeling... confused. And maybe a little stupid. Empathy? Connection? I thought punk was about being loud and pissed off. I thought competitions were about winning. Leo and Gemini... sometimes it felt like they were playing a completely different game than I was. A game with rules I didn't understand and stakes that felt way too high.

Practice that night felt... off. Way off. We were back in Jessica's ridiculously huge garage, the familiar smell of dusty amps usually comforting, but tonight the air felt thick, strained.

The easy vibe from before the audition, even the defiant energy after we decided to enter, felt like it had evaporated, replaced by a weird, prickly tension. Jessica seemed jumpy as hell, constantly checking her phone between songs, her playing technically perfect, as always, but lacking its usual soul, like she was just going through the motions. Gemini was even quieter than usual, withdrawn, spending ages tweaking the knobs on her bass amp, fiddling with cables, avoiding eye contact. When she did speak, it was clipped, critical. Leo kept trying to inject upbeat ska riffs into everything, like he could force the mood to lift through sheer trumpet power, but even his energy felt forced, brittle, stretched too thin. Only Mack seemed the same, laying down steady, precise beats from behind her kit, her face impassive, watching us all with those unnervingly calm, observant eyes. Sometimes I felt like she was the only adult in the room, just waiting for the rest of us kids to stop squabbling.

"Okay, so, next round," I said, trying to inject some positive energy after a particularly messy run-through of an older, faster song where everyone seemed to be playing in a different time zone. "The Quarterfinals. This is where it gets serious. We need something strong. Something that shows off our chops. What about that instrumental break we worked on a while back? The one with the dueling guitar and trumpet? It's complex, shows we can really play." I looked around, hoping for agreement.

Gemini stopped tuning her bass mid-note, the string twanging slightly. "It's not about 'chops,' Rhys," she said, her voice flat. "It's about the song. The message. What are we trying to *say*?"

"We're trying to say we're good enough to win!" I argued, frustration rising. "The judges *liked* the technical stuff! That guy literally said 'technically proficient'! We need to lean into that!"

"He also said 'raw'," Gemini countered dryly, finally looking at me. "Which I'm pretty sure was code for 'needs corporate sanitizing'. Playing some wanky instrumental isn't going to cut it. We need substance."

"Maybe we write something new?" Leo suggested, his eyes brightening slightly, seizing the opening. "Something that really says something about what's happening *now*? About the 'Family Harmony Act' maybe? Something topical?"

Jessica visibly flinched, her head snapping up, eyes wide with something that looked like panic. "No!" she said, too quickly, too sharply. "Absolutely not. Too risky, Leo. Way too political. Sal already warned us about causing trouble. And... and we need something the judges will actually *like*. Something... accessible." She looked down, fiddling with her guitar pick.

"Accessible?" Gemini raised a skeptical eyebrow. "Since when are *we* accessible, Jess?"

"Look, we need to be strategic!" I insisted, feeling that familiar frustration bubble up again. Why couldn't they see it? We were finally getting somewhere, and they wanted to throw it away on politics or obscure musical choices. "This is a competition! We need to play the game a little if we want to advance. We need a song that connects! Maybe even a cover? Something people recognize?"

"A cover?" Gemini looked genuinely horrified, like I'd suggested sacrificing a goat on stage. "Absolutely not. We play our own music."

"Why not?" I demanded, exasperated. "Lots of bands do covers! It shows range!"

"We're not 'lots of bands'," she said flatly, turning away again.

"Okay, okay," Jessica cut in quickly, holding up her hands like a referee trying to stop a fight. "No covers. Fine. But maybe... maybe something less... intense than 'Torn to Shreds'? Something that shows our musicality without being... abrasive? We need to show versatility." She avoided looking at Gemini as she said it.

"Versatility?" Leo scoffed, crossing his arms. "Or conformity?"

"It's called strategy!" I said, louder than I intended, my voice cracking slightly. "It's called trying to *win*! Isn't that the point of a competition?"

"Winning isn't the point!" Gemini snapped, whirling back around, her eyes flashing with anger.

"Then what *is* the point, Gemini?" I shot back, tired of being dismissed, tired of the negativity. "Just getting kicked out? Making some big political statement nobody hears because SNN cuts our feed five seconds in? What good does that do?"

The silence that followed was heavy, suffocating. Mack stopped drumming, the sudden absence of rhythm deafening. Leo looked away, shaking his head slightly. Jessica stared fixedly at her guitar strings like they held the secrets to the universe. Gemini just glared at me, her expression a mixture of anger and something that looked disappointingly like pity.

"The point," she said finally, her voice dangerously quiet, each word precise, "is to not sell our souls for a chance to lick Sterling's boots. The point is to say something true, even if nobody with power wants to hear it. The point is to not become the plastic, smiling puppets they want us to be." She held my gaze for a beat longer, then turned back to her amp, fiddling with the knobs. "Let's just run the set list we have for the next round. We'll figure out the new song later. Or not."

Practice ended soon after that, the air thick with unspoken arguments and resentment. As we were packing up our gear, I saw Gemini talking quietly with Mack by the drum kit, gesturing towards her bass, then glancing over at me. Probably complaining about my playing again, or my attitude. Whatever. I focused on meticulously cleaning my fretboard with lemon oil, feeling that familiar, hot sting of being excluded, misunderstood. They just didn't get it. This wasn't just some gig at The Rat Hole where you could play whatever angry noise you wanted. This was a real shot. A chance to get noticed, to get signed, to get *out*. And they were going to blow it with all their politics and negativity.

Walking back to my dorm later that night, the GLAMA air cool against my face, I pulled up the SNN highlight reel from the first prelims on my phone again. There was Iron Eagle, looking powerful and professional under the bright stage lights, the edited crowd noise making it sound like a stadium was roaring its approval. They looked like winners. Like they knew how to play the game.

Maybe, I thought, kicking a loose pebble on the sidewalk, maybe *they* had the right idea after all. Focus on the music, the power, the professionalism. Give the people – and the judges, and the sponsors – what they want. That's how you get ahead. That's how you win. This Freedom's Ring thing... it felt important. It felt like *my* chance. I just hoped the rest of the band wouldn't screw it up before we even really got started. We needed a plan. We needed a strategy. We needed to stop fighting amongst ourselves and start playing the game.

CHAPTER 6: GEMINI

The week following the first preliminary round felt like wading through lukewarm sludge. We'd advanced – the official Freedom's Ring portal confirmed it with a sterile, algorithmically generated message – but the victory felt hollow, tainted. The whole experience replayed in my head on a loop: the beige corporate holding room smelling faintly of bleach and fear; the dead-eyed judges tapping on their Sterling™ tablets; the impassive red lights of the SNN cameras; Rick Anderson, the perfectly tailored producer, cornering Jessica with his veiled threats wrapped in professional courtesy; Kane Krieger spitting that racist, dismissive insult. Low-rent island import trash. The words echoed, ugly and sticky.

What were we even *doing* here? My decision to enter, that flash of reactive anger sparked by Krieger's bullshit, felt thin and shaky in the harsh light of day. We played their game, walked onto their stage, offered up our music – *our* music – for their judgment, and got... what? Three blurry seconds in a propaganda montage designed to make Sterling look benevolent, and a warning delivered via Jessica's family connections that left her pale and jumpy for days? It felt less like fighting back and more like willingly participating in our own neutering, handing them the scissors ourselves. Had I dragged us into this cage just because some fascist asshole pushed my buttons? It felt stupid. Naive. Exactly the kind of mistake I usually prided myself on avoiding.

Practice was tense. Excruciatingly so. The easy flow we sometimes found in Jessica's garage, that magical space where four disparate people somehow locked into the same rhythm, the same feeling, felt completely blocked, dammed up by unspoken anxieties and conflicting agendas. Jessica was quiet, withdrawn, picking at her guitar strings between songs, her playing technically brilliant but emotionally guarded, like she was afraid to let anything real slip through the cracks in her perfect facade. The producer's words had clearly hit their mark, reinforcing whatever fears were already swirling inside her. Leo vibrated with frustrated energy, wanting to push harder, say more, his trumpet lines sharper, more aggressive, but he seemed hesitant to push Jessica too far, sensing her fragility. And Rhys... Rhys was living in a different reality altogether. He was buzzing about viewer counts on the SNN clips (our three seconds apparently got replayed!), talking strategy, suggesting maybe we should "lean into the energy" but "smooth out the rough edges" for the next round. He even brought up covers again, completely oblivious – or willfully ignorant – to the tightening knot of dread in my stomach or the shadows under Jessica's eyes. His relentless focus on *winning*, on viewing this whole farce as a legitimate career opportunity, felt like sandpaper scraping against my last nerve. Didn't he hear anything we actually sang about? Did he even listen to the words, or just the chord progressions and the potential for fame?

That argument after practice... "Winning isn't the point!" I'd snapped, the words sharper than I intended. But watching Rhys's genuinely bewildered face ("Then what *is* the point?"), seeing Jessica flinch away from the conflict, hearing Leo's sigh of frustration... maybe I wasn't getting it right either. What *was* the point, if we couldn't even agree on that? If playing music together, the one thing that usually felt true and clear, now just exposed the widening cracks between us? Even my impulsive decision to enter the competition, partly fueled by a desire to maybe, somehow, force a connection, force *something* real, felt like it had backfired, pushing us further apart.

I retreated to my room after another particularly grating lecture on post-structuralism, the professor's jargon about the instability of meaning feeling ironically, painfully relevant. Flopped onto my mattress, sketchbook open, pen hovering over a blank page. I couldn't draw. The images wouldn't come. Only the static. The feeling of disconnect, of misalignment. Like watching the world through warped, cracked glass, seeing things distorted, unable to agree on basic colors, basic truths. Were we all looking at the same stage, the same city, the same creeping threat, but through entirely different lenses?

Static hums behind the glass...

Watching shadows flicker past...

You say blue, I see it gray...

Words get twisted on the way...

The lines came first, fragmented, mirroring the fractured feeling inside. I picked up my bass, not bothering with the amp, just feeling the familiar weight, the vibration of the strings against my fingers as I plucked out a hesitant rhythm. A bassline started to emerge, not the heavy dub anchor I often defaulted to, but something more anxious, driving, dissonant. A nervous energy pulsed in the rhythm, a question mark hanging in the minor key phrasing. Post-punk paranoia.

Hear the echo, read the feed...

Planting doubt like poison seed...

Smiling faces on the screen...

Selling worlds I've never seen...

It wasn't just about the band, about Rhys's infuriating blindness or Jessica's understandable fear, or even Leo's righteous anger. It was bigger than us. It was the SNN broadcasts smoothing over police brutality, calling protests 'disturbances.' It was the online forums twisting facts into unrecognizable shapes, amplifying hate under the guise of 'free speech.' It was the way people on campus could look at the same event, the same oppressive policy, and see completely different things depending on the lens they wore – privilege, fear, ideology, willful ignorance. Like we were all living in slightly different, incompatible realities, beamed directly into our heads by competing narratives.

We're looking through different lenses now...

Cracked reflections, anyhow...

The picture's blurred, the focus gone...

Can't agree on dusk or dawn...

The melody taking shape in my head felt tense, angular, unresolved. I imagined Jessica's guitar playing sharp, stabbing chords against my driving, slightly off-kilter bassline. Leo's trumpet wouldn't be bright ska here; it would be sparse, discordant stabs, maybe echoing feedback, adding to the paranoia, the feeling of signals crossing, interfering. *This distorted frequency... Is it them, or is it me?* The question hung there, heavy and unsettling. Was I the only one seeing the cracks widening, the static overwhelming the signal? Or was I just projecting my own cynicism onto everything, unable to see the 'opportunity' Rhys was so desperate for?

Little fractures start to spread...

Arguments inside my head...

You hear comfort, I hear lies...

Behind those calculated eyes...

I scribbled furiously in my notebook, lyrics and chord notations blurring together on the page, the pen digging into the paper. It wasn't a protest song, not directly like some of our others. It wasn't a call to arms. It was a snapshot of the confusion, the breakdown in communication, the feeling of reality itself becoming unstable, unreliable. *Different Lenses.* Yeah. That felt right. It felt honest, at least. It wasn't finished, not by a long shot, the bridge felt weak, the outro nonexistent, but the core was there. Maybe… maybe this was something we could actually play. Something that captured the *feeling* of being inside this machine, navigating this distorted landscape, without starting another unwinnable argument about tactics. Maybe this was the way to talk about the static without just adding more noise.

Bringing a new song to the band always felt like ripping off a Band-Aid. Especially now. I waited until near the end of our next practice, after we'd listlessly run through "Torn to Shreds" and a couple of older tracks. The air in Jessica's garage was still thick with unspoken tension.

"So," I started, trying to sound casual, holding up my lyric-scribbled notebook page. "I was messing around with something new. Based on… well, based on how weird everything feels right now. How nobody seems to be seeing the same thing."

Rhys immediately perked up. "New song? Awesome! Is it fast? We need something high-energy for the next round!"

I ignored him, looking at Jessica and Leo. "It's called 'Different Lenses.' It's… uh… more post-punk, maybe? A bit angular." I hesitated. "It's about the disconnect. The static."

Leo frowned slightly, tilting his head. "Different lenses… like how the media twists things?"

"Yeah," I said. "And… other stuff. How people see things differently depending on… you know." I glanced quickly at Jessica, who was studiously examining her fretboard.

"Let's hear it," Mack said quietly from behind the kit, her voice cutting through the awkward silence.

My hands felt sweaty on the bass neck. I took a breath and started playing the anxious, driving bassline, nodding to Mack to pick up the slightly off-kilter beat. I sang the first verse, my voice feeling thin and exposed in the relative quiet.

Static hums behind the glass…

Watching shadows flicker past...

You say blue, I see it gray...

Words get twisted on the way...

Jessica started picking out hesitant, dissonant chords on her guitar, her brow furrowed in concentration, listening. Leo lifted his trumpet but didn't play yet, just watched me, his expression thoughtful. Rhys looked slightly confused, probably waiting for the big, dumb rock riff.

I pushed through the chorus, the words feeling raw and true. *We're looking through different lenses now... Cracked reflections, anyhow...*

As I finished the second verse, Jessica seemed to find the groove, her guitar chords becoming sharper, more confident, locking in with my bass and Mack's tense rhythm. Leo started adding short, sharp trumpet stabs, perfectly capturing the feeling of paranoia, of signals breaking up. Even Rhys seemed to catch on, adding a layer of scratchy rhythm guitar that actually fit the mood.

We stumbled through the structure I'd sketched out, finding our way through the changes, the tension building in the instrumental break. It wasn't perfect, far from it, but for the first time all week, it felt like we were actually playing *together*, channeling the shared frustration and confusion into something coherent, something *ours*.

When we finished, the silence felt different this time. Not empty, but charged.

"Whoa," Rhys said, actually sounding impressed. "That's... different. Kinda dark. I like the weird rhythm."

"Yeah," Leo agreed, nodding slowly. "Yeah, I feel that. Distorted frequency... that hits." He looked at me. "Needs a bridge, though. And a better outro."

"I know," I admitted. "It's still rough."

"But it's good, Gem," Jessica said softly, finally meeting my eyes. There was still caution there, but also a spark of connection I hadn't seen all week. "It feels... real."

A small knot of tension eased in my chest. Maybe this could work. Maybe this song was a way forward, a way to acknowledge the cracks without shattering completely. "So... we work on it?" I asked. "For the Quarterfinals?"

There were nods around the room. Even Rhys seemed genuinely on board this time, maybe intrigued by the musical challenge. For the next hour, we hammered away at "Different Lenses," fleshing out the structure, tightening the transitions, Leo experimenting with horn lines for the bridge, Jessica adding layers of spiky guitar texture. It felt productive. It felt like us again.

The next afternoon found me back in the library, ostensibly studying Foucault but mostly staring out the window at the relentlessly cheerful campus quad. Practice last night had felt... okay. Better, anyway. We actually sounded like a band again working on "Different Lenses." It wasn't a fiery protest anthem, but it felt honest, like something that captured the weird, fractured mood of the moment. It felt like *us*.

With a sigh, I pulled my laptop towards me, pushing Foucault aside. Might as well make it official. I logged into the Freedom's Ring competitor portal – another sleek, Sterling-branded interface, all sharp lines and corporate blue. Navigated through the upcoming Quarterfinal round requirements. *Song Submission Deadline: Friday.* Okay, still had a couple of days, but might as well get it over with while the fragile band unity felt relatively intact.

I typed in the song title: *Different Lenses.* Uploaded the rough demo we'd recorded on Jessica's phone during practice – just enough for them to get the gist. Checked the box confirming it was an original composition. Hesitated for a second before clicking 'Submit'. It felt weirdly final. Locking us into playing this anxious, questioning song on Sterling's big, shiny stage. Was it the right move? Was it enough? Or was it just another small compromise, another step into the cage?

Screw it. I clicked Submit. The portal flashed a confirmation message: "Thank You for Your Submission! Unleash Your Voice!" I closed the laptop lid with a snap, feeling a strange mix of relief and unease. Done. We were committed. Now we just had to survive playing it.

I was still sitting there, trying to force myself to read about disciplinary power, when my phone started buzzing uncontrollably on the table, vibrating against the wood like an angry insect. Then Leo's phone across the room started buzzing too. Then other phones around the library. A ripple of digital alarm spreading through the quiet space. Texts flooded in – from Leo, from activist groups I followed, from friends I hadn't heard from in months. Links to independent news sites, frantic all-caps messages: *DID YOU SEE?? THEY ACTUALLY DID IT! WTF SCOTUS??*

I clicked the first link Leo sent, my blood going cold as I read the headline, the words blurring together. They'd actually done it. The deceptively named "Family Harmony Act," a piece of legislation I remembered SNN relentlessly promoting for months, pushed through Congress by a razor-thin margin after an election cycle heavily influenced by Sterling's media empire, and signed into law by a President who owed him more than a few favors, had finally survived its last legal challenge. The newly stacked Supreme Court – packed with judges Sterling's networks had championed through manufactured public pressure campaigns ("Write-In for Righteousness!") and backroom political deals – had just overturned decades of precedent to uphold it. Citing obscure historical texts selectively interpreted through a lens of bigotry, and invoking the hollow phrase "traditional values," they'd effectively abolished legal recognition and protection for same-sex relationships nationwide. Just like that. Decades of progress, erased with the stroke of a few pens wielded by men (mostly men) whose confirmation hearings felt like exercises in doublespeak and bad faith. The entire machinery of the state, greased by Sterling's money and amplified by his voice, had delivered for its benefactor.

The library, usually a haven of quiet concentration, felt suddenly too quiet, the air thick and suffocating. My hands were shaking as I scrolled through the initial analysis, the dry legalese barely masking the profound cruelty, the deliberate targeting. This wasn't abstract political theory anymore. This wasn't someone else's problem I could analyze with academic detachment for Professor Davies. This was me. This was Jessica. Our relationship, the tentative, unspoken, fragile thing blooming between us, the thing that felt like the only real anchor in my increasingly chaotic life – it wasn't just frowned upon by her parents or complicated by our different backgrounds anymore. It was *illegal*. Retroactively dangerous. A potential crime under the law of the land. Every shared glance, every lingering touch, every late-night conversation suddenly felt weighted with a new, terrifying significance. The simple act of writing her name inside a heart in my notebook felt like composing evidence.

My first instinct was panic, a cold wave washing over me that left me breathless, dizzy. My second was fury, hot and blinding, a rage so intense it made my vision blur, made the words on the screen swim. *This Machine Kills Fascists.* The sticker on my bass wasn't just a slogan anymore. It felt less like a historical reference and more like a burning, desperate imperative.

And then came the third wave, colder and sharper than the panic: guilt. What was I doing, waiting for Jessica? I knew how she felt, I saw it in her eyes sometimes, felt it in the way she leaned just a little too close when we were working on a song, the way her fingers brushed mine when she passed me a pick. And she had to know how I felt; "Free to Be" wasn't exactly subtle, even if she pretended not to get the second verse. But she wasn't ready. Scared of her parents, scared of the world, maybe scared of herself. And I'd been patient, telling myself it was okay to wait, to give her space. But now? Now waiting felt… dangerous. Irresponsible. Was I putting her at risk just by *being* near her, by letting this unspoken thing linger? Was it fair to dangle this possibility, this future that was now actively criminalized, in front of her when she was already terrified?

Did our relationship even *need* to be more intimate, more defined, to be real? Wasn't our friendship, our musical connection, enough? God, I didn't know. I was nineteen, barely an adult, trying to navigate a world that seemed determined to legislate my heart out of existence. How was I supposed to know the 'right' way to love someone, especially now? The stakes felt impossibly high, and my own certainty, my usual cynical clarity, felt completely inadequate.

I looked up from my phone, scanning the faces around me in the library, feeling profoundly alone. Most students were still engrossed in their laptops, oblivious, inhabiting a different reality where court decisions didn't fundamentally alter their right to exist. A few were clustered together near the windows, whispering anxiously, faces pale. Others scrolled through their phones, their expressions ranging from shock to anger to… indifference. That casual indifference, the ability to just scroll past, was almost the worst part. It was the fertile ground where fascism took root.

On the official news feeds later that day, the spin machine kicked into high gear. SNN framed the ruling as a victory for "states' rights," "democracy," and "protecting the traditional family," interviewing carefully selected "experts" and religious figures who praised the court's "courage" and "return to foundational principles." Any mention of lost rights or the ruling's impact on actual human beings was buried under layers of patriotic rhetoric and legalistic jargon. Online, the comment sections were a predictable cesspool of triumphant bigotry, whataboutism, and bots spewing coordinated talking points, drowning out the voices of pain and outrage. It was a masterclass in how Sterling used his platform, his voice, to shape reality, to tell people what to think and how to feel, drowning out any inconvenient truths with a firehose of curated narratives.

At university the next day, the atmosphere was subdued but fractured. Avoided eyes. Awkward silences in hallways. Some students in my Poli Sci class, mostly the Chad Broleton types, parroted the SNN talking points about "judicial restraint" and "respecting the constitution," their voices full of the unearned confidence that came from never having their existence debated by strangers in robes. Others, mostly queer kids or those with friends directly impacted, looked shell-shocked, angry, scared, moving through the halls like ghosts. Many just looked uncomfortable, changing the subject quickly, retreating into the safety of coursework or campus gossip. The normalization was happening in real time, the initial shock already fading into weary acceptance or deliberate ignorance for those unaffected. The frog was boiling, and half the people in the pot didn't even seem to notice the water getting hotter.

I called Mom that night, bracing myself for the inevitable deflection, needing, foolishly, some sign that my own family wasn't completely submerged in the propaganda. "Did you hear about the Court decision?" I asked, trying to keep the tremor out of my voice. "Oh, that? Yes, terrible business," she said, her voice distracted. I could hear the clatter of dishes in the background. "Sounds very complicated. Your father was reading about it, says it's mostly political grandstanding, probably won't change much practically for most people. Are you remembering to eat properly, sweetie? You sounded thin last time we talked." *Political grandstanding. Won't change much practically.* My teeth clenched so hard my jaw ached. Easy for her to say from the safety of her heterosexual marriage in the suburbs. Easy for her to believe the soothing lies on SNN. The disconnect felt like a physical chasm opening between us. "Yeah, Mom," I managed. "Eating fine." I ended the call quickly, the familiar ache of disappointment settling in my chest.

Practice that night was brutal. The unspoken tension from before had coalesced into something heavy, suffocating, poisonous. Jessica arrived late, her eyes red-rimmed and puffy, avoiding looking directly at me or anyone else. She tuned her guitar with trembling fingers, her usual meticulous care replaced by jerky, uncertain movements. Leo was vibrating with a barely suppressed rage, pacing the confines of the garage like a caged tiger, muttering curses under his breath in a mixture of English and French. Even Mack seemed different, her usual stoicism overlaid with a grim tightness around her jaw, her drumsticks tapping a restless, angry rhythm against her thigh.

Only Rhys seemed unchanged, utterly oblivious to the emotional storm swirling around him. He launched into a discussion about the online reaction to our SNN clip as soon as he plugged in his guitar. "People are saying we need a stronger image!" he announced cheerfully, adjusting his strap. "You know, more cohesive? Maybe some matching outfits? Like, black jeans and band shirts?"

Leo stopped pacing mid-stride, whirling around to face Rhys, his face incredulous. "Matching outfits?" he repeated, his voice dangerously low. "Are you fucking kidding me, Rhys? Did you even *see* the news today? Do you have any idea what just happened?"

Rhys looked genuinely bewildered, glancing between Leo's furious face and Jessica's tear-streaked one. "What news? Oh, that court thing? Yeah, wild. Terrible. But what does that have to do with band outfits? We need to look professional for the next round!"

"What does it–?" Leo sputtered, his voice rising, losing the battle for control. "It has *everything* to do with it! They're outlawing people's lives, Rhys! They're coming for anyone who doesn't fit their perfect little mold! They're telling people like Gem, people like me eventually, that we don't belong, that we have no rights! And you're worried about *fucking outfits*?"

"Hey, I'm just saying what people online are saying!" Rhys

protested defensively, taking a step back. "We need to think about our brand if we want to get noticed! It's not political, it's just marketing!"

"Our brand?" I finally spoke, my voice quiet but vibrating with a cold fury I hadn't known I possessed. My blue mohawk probably bristled. "Our *brand* is staring down fascists, Rhys. Or it's supposed to be. Our *brand* is the goddamn sticker on my bass. It's not about marketing; it's about survival."

"But winning–" Rhys started, falling back on his usual refrain.

"FUCK WINNING!" Leo exploded, slamming his fist against the side of Jessica's Marshall amp with a loud, reverberating thud. Jessica flinched violently, tears finally spilling over, running silently down her cheeks. "This isn't about winning some stupid corporate talent show anymore!" Leo raged, his voice choked with emotion. "This is about fighting back before there's nothing left to fight for! Don't you get it?"

Jessica let out a small, broken sob. "Can we just… can we just play?" she whispered, her voice trembling. "Please? Just play something?"

The fight went out of Leo instantly. He looked at Jessica's pale, tear-streaked face, then at me, his anger collapsing into a weary, shared understanding of the impossible situation we were in. Mack, who had been watching silently, started a slow, heavy beat, a funeral dirge for rights revoked. We tried to play "Different Lenses," the song that had felt like a step forward just days before, the one we'd officially submitted, but the anxious energy now felt laughably inadequate, the lyrics about subtle distortions meaningless in the face of this blatant assault. The music was ragged, discordant, falling apart before the first chorus. The cracks between us felt like gaping chasms, impossible to bridge with just noise. We gave up quickly, the silence returning, heavier than before.

Later, back in my cramped room, the frustration and fury and fear churning inside me like toxic sludge, I pulled out my sketchbook again. "Different Lenses" felt like a relic from another era, written before the ground shifted beneath our feet. It felt inadequate now. Too subtle. Too internal. Too... polite. This new reality, this blatant attack, required something else. Something louder. Angrier. More direct. A weapon, not just an observation. Playing that song in the Quarterfinals now felt like bringing a strongly worded letter to a gunfight. But we were locked in. Too late to switch now. The fury needed an outlet, though, before it consumed me, before I said or did something that shattered the band completely.

My pen flew across the page, words pouring out, fueled by the court decision, by Rhys's willful blindness, by Jessica's devastating fear, by Leo's righteous rage, by the slick lies on SNN, by the smug, untouchable face of Sterling plastered everywhere.

Same old story, different screen...

Selling nightmares, calling dreams...

Got your flag wrapped tight and clean...

Hide the dirt that lies between!

The rhythm pounding in my head wasn't ska, wasn't reggae, wasn't even really punk. It was heavier, angrier, more relentless. A driving, almost metallic bassline. Guitars like jagged shards of glass. A pounding drumbeat like Mack's controlled fury unleashed.

Billionaire kings on gilded thrones...

Chewing futures, sucking bones...

Got your mouthpiece? Yeah, it drones!

While you tap your shiny phones!

This wasn't subtle. This wasn't coded. This was a Molotov cocktail in lyrical form, aimed directly at the heart of the machine.

THIS! Is your Patriot Games!

Twisting truth and whispering names!

Yeah. *Patriot Games.* That felt right. That felt necessary. This wouldn't be for the Quarterfinals. This was for later. This was for the *real* fight. If we even made it that far. Writing it down felt like packing ammunition, even if I didn't know when or if I'd get to fire the gun. It was the only thing I could do right now besides scream.

CHAPTER 7: LEO LIEFSON

The trumpet felt cold against my lips, heavy and useless in my hands, like a dead weight. Even in the stuffy, sunbaked heat of my tiny dorm room overlooking a concrete courtyard littered with cigarette butts and discarded vape cartridges, a chill seeped into my bones, raising goosebumps on my arms.

I tried running through some scales, the familiar warm-up routine, the simple patterns of notes that usually centered me, calmed the buzzing in my head. But today, the notes felt flat, lifeless, sour. My fingers fumbled on the valves, clumsy and unresponsive, slick with a nervous sweat. My breath kept catching in my chest, shallow and tight, like I'd run a mile uphill carrying an amplifier. It had been like this for days, ever since the news about the "Family Harmony Act" dropped like a concrete block into the already churning cesspool of GLAMA politics, sending shockwaves of fear and anger through the communities I was just starting to feel a part of.

Family Harmony. What a fucking joke. Orwell would be taking notes. More like State-Sanctioned Hate, wrapped in a flag and delivered with a folksy smile by the SNN anchors. Every time I thought about it, saw the smug, self-satisfied pronouncements on the ever-present screens around campus, heard the casual bigotry it unleashed echoing like poison gas in dining halls and lecture queues – "Well, it's about protecting traditional marriage," "They just want special rights," "It's always been this way, really" – a cold dread seeped deeper, chilling me despite the relentless sunshine beating down outside my window.

It wasn't just about marriage equality, not really. I knew, Gemini knew, anyone paying attention knew – it was just the next step. Another group targeted, another freedom chipped away under the guise of tradition and order and "safety." They build the cage bar by bar. First, they came hard for the immigrants, especially those from south of the border – tightening border controls that were already brutal, increasing sweeps and raids by the CPB – the Citizen Protection Bureau, another Orwellian name for Sterling's increasingly powerful, black-uniformed internal security force – making people constantly look over their shoulders, jump at unexpected knocks on the door, live in perpetual fear of deportation to places they barely knew or had fled in terror. Now, this. Targeting love itself, drawing another arbitrary line between acceptable citizens and disposable deviants. Who was next? Artists? Activists? People with the wrong skin color, the wrong religion, the wrong thoughts? Anyone who didn't fit the mold Sterling was pouring for his new, compliant GLAMA? The list felt like it was getting longer every single day.

My breath hitched again, the memory flashing sharp and unwelcome behind my eyes, vivid as if it were yesterday morning: the blinding glare of headlights pinning me against a graffitied wall after that housing rights protest last year. The rough hands shoving me hard, face scraping against cold, gritty brick. The sickening, ratcheting click of zip ties biting into my wrists, cinching tight enough to cut off circulation. The officer's bored, contemptuous voice spitting out accusations – *inciting unrest, resisting arrest, violation of student visa terms* – just for being there. Just for holding a sign that said "No Human Is Illegal." Just for being in the wrong place with the wrong face when the crackdown order came down. I'd spent twelve hours crammed into a crowded, stinking holding cell, the air thick with fear and despair, the metallic tang of blood from someone's split lip, listening to hushed stories of families separated, terrified they'd deport me on the spot, terrified my parents back in Toronto would get that dreaded middle-of-the-night call.

They let me go eventually, some bureaucratic oversight or maybe just couldn't be bothered with the paperwork for a Canadian kid when they had bigger targets, just a warning scribbled on some official form and a new, permanent flag on my digital file. But the fear never really left. The feeling of being powerless, disposable, marked. A guest whose welcome could be revoked at any moment, for any reason, however arbitrary. And now, seeing the same mechanisms of the state, the same dehumanizing rhetoric, the same 'othering' tactics turned against Gem and Jessica, against countless others whose only crime was loving who they loved... it wasn't just triggering; it felt like the walls were physically closing in on all of us. This wasn't Canada. The assumptions of basic fairness, the belief in due process I'd grown up with – they didn't apply here, not anymore, maybe they never really did for people who looked like Gemini, or people who didn't have the right papers, like me.

I put the trumpet down gently on my narrow bed, wiping sweaty palms on my brightly colored cargo pants. The usual upbeat ska rhythms that usually bounced around in my head, my internal soundtrack of defiant optimism, were gone, replaced by a frantic, anxious energy, a buzzing static that made it hard to think straight, hard to breathe. I needed to move, needed to *do* something. Sitting here practicing scales while the world outside burned felt... wrong. Pointless. Masturbatory. Like polishing brass on the Titanic.

Before heading out, on a grim impulse I immediately regretted, I logged into my GLAMA U student portal, navigating through the labyrinthine menus, the cheerful university branding feeling like a sick joke. International Student Services. Visa Status. My heart hammered against my ribs as the page loaded. The usual reassuring green checkmark was gone. Replaced by a flashing yellow warning triangle, stark against the white background.

"Status Under Review. Please ensure all documentation is up-to-date per CPB Mandate 7.4b. Additional biometric verification may be required. Failure to comply promptly with CPB requests may impact your enrollment and residency status." Vague. Threatening. No specific request, just… a warning. A digital leash, reminding me to behave, reminding me of my precariousness. My stomach churned. It hadn't said that last week. Mandate 7.4b? What the hell was that? Probably some new regulation buried in fine print, designed to catch people like me unawares.

I slammed the laptop shut, the click echoing too loudly in the small room. Grabbed my keys, shoved my wallet in my pocket, and bolted out of the dorm, needing air, needing noise, needing anything but the suffocating silence of my room and the cold, menacing glow of that warning message. I ended up wandering east again, instinctively seeking distance from the manicured lawns and Sterling-sponsored "excellence" of the campus, needing the grit and honesty, even the ugliness, of the city streets. The further east I walked, the more the city's mask slipped. The Sterling Security™ signs vanished, replaced by peeling flyers for tenants' rights meetings taped to lampposts, handwritten notices seeking missing family members, and faded graffiti demanding justice – *"Justicia Ahora!" "Who Elected Sterling?" "Where Did They Go?"* The streets were cracked here, the storefronts often boarded up or protected by heavy metal grates, but there was a different kind of energy too – a resilience, a simmering anger, a sense of community forged in shared struggle that felt more real, more alive, than anything on the privileged, insulated campus grounds. People looked out for each other here, shared information in hushed tones, kept watch.

Turning a corner onto a narrow side street lined with auto body shops and shuttered warehouses, I saw it. Scrawled hastily in bright blue spray paint across a corrugated metal fence, stark against the rust and grime: *Free to Be?* The question mark felt deliberate, defiant. My steps faltered. *Free to Be.* Our song. Or maybe just the sentiment, bubbling up from the collective unconscious of the oppressed city. Did it matter? Seeing those words there, scrawled in the heart of the struggle, felt like a jolt, a spark in the suffocating darkness. Someone else felt it. Someone else was asking the question. Maybe we weren't just screaming into the void after all. A small, fierce flicker of hope ignited in my chest, quickly banked by caution, but there nonetheless.

Near Mariachi Plaza, under the faded arches where musicians usually gathered, hoping for gigs, their vibrant music a defiant counterpoint to the surrounding decay, I saw them – two GLAMA PD cruisers parked aggressively on the sidewalk, lights flashing unnecessarily, casting lurid red and blue strobes across the faces of nervous bystanders. Two officers, puffed up with authority, helmets reflecting the harsh sunlight, were hassling a couple of street vendors selling fruit from a brightly painted cart. Just hassling them, demanding permits I knew they probably had, speaking too loudly in condescending, deliberately slow English, enjoying the power imbalance, making a public spectacle of their dominance. One officer knocked over a small stack of mangoes with deliberate carelessness. It wasn't a raid, not exactly, but it was intimidation. It was the state making its presence felt, reminding everyone who was in charge, who belonged and who didn't, who could be pushed around with impunity. *Orderly compliance.* It was the same tactic they used at protests, the same casual dehumanization, just applied to people trying to make a living. Seeing it, feeling the familiar knot of helpless fear and righteous anger tighten in my gut, solidified something in me. We couldn't just play their game. We couldn't just be "accessible." We couldn't afford to be subtle anymore. This wasn't just background static; this was the boot on the neck, pressing down harder every day.

That conviction carried me into practice later that week, but the atmosphere in Jessica's garage felt like walking into a minefield. The air was thick with unspoken things, heavy with Jessica's palpable fear and Gemini's tightly coiled fury. Rhys, bless his oblivious heart, was chattering about online comments about our band needing a "stronger image," completely missing the emotional storm brewing around him. When Jessica, pale and withdrawn, started pushing nervously for us to play something "safer" than "Different Lenses" for the Quarterfinals, something "less likely to cause waves," I couldn't stay quiet. Playing it safe felt like a betrayal, not just of our music, but of everything happening outside this privileged, soundproofed garage.

"Accessible? Are you kidding me, Jess?" The words burst out before I could stop them.

"We have 'Different Lenses'," I argued, trying to keep my voice steady, trying to channel the anger I felt into conviction, not just noise. I knew we'd submitted it, locked it in on that damn portal just before the court ruling dropped. "It's a good song! It says something! But maybe... maybe it's not enough anymore? After the court ruling? After seeing how they operate out there?" I gestured vaguely towards the door, towards the city beyond the manicured lawns.

"What are you saying, Leo?" Gem asked, her eyes sharp, watching me closely. She knew where this was going.

"I'm saying maybe we need to be louder!" I finally let it out, the frustration and fear boiling over. "Maybe 'Different Lenses' is too subtle now! It talks about static, about confusion – fine! But they just declared war on love! My god, Gem, they just made it illegal for you and—" I cut myself off abruptly, seeing Jessica flinch, her face paling even further, seeing the sudden warning flash in Gem's eyes. Shit. Too far. Too real. I quickly pivoted, the unspoken hanging heavy in the air, thick with Jessica's terror. "They declared war on basic human rights!" I continued, my voice maybe a little too loud now, trying to cover the stumble. "Maybe we need to hit them harder! Why are we playing *their* game, walking on eggshells, trying to be 'accessible'?" I gestured wildly with my hands, needing to make them understand. "Look what's happening! They're stripping rights away piece by piece, they're targeting people – queer people, immigrants, anyone who doesn't fit their perfect little mold! They're using this whole competition – this 'Freedom's Ring' bullshit – as a fucking propaganda machine, and we're worried about being *abrasive*?"

"It's strategy, Leo!" Rhys interjected, ever the pragmatist (or maybe just the opportunist, focused only on the prize). "We have to get through the rounds first! We can't make a statement if we get disqualified!"

"What good is getting through if we sound like fucking Heartwood by the end?" I shot back, referencing the folk band whose traditional sound felt completely neutered and co-opted by the competition's patriotic framing. "What good is a platform if we say nothing real with it? If we just become another part of the background noise? Another Sterling-approved jingle?"

"Leo's right," Gemini said quietly, surprising me. Her eyes met mine, a shared understanding passing between us – the recognition that the game had changed, that subtlety might be a luxury we could no longer afford. "Playing it safe feels... wrong now. 'Different Lenses' felt right last week. This week? After the ruling?" She shook her head, her expression grim. "It feels like whispering when we need to scream."

"But we submitted it!" Jessica cried, her voice cracking, tears welling in her eyes. The fear radiating off her was palpable, almost suffocating. "We can't change it now! And... and what about what Anderson said? That producer? About my family? We can't just... provoke them! Don't you understand what could happen?"

"So we let them silence us?" I asked, my voice rising again, fueled by a desperate need to make her see, to make them *all* see the connection. "We let them threaten your family into making us toothless? That's how it works, Jess! That's how they win! They isolate, they intimidate, they make you afraid to speak! They make *us* afraid to stand up for each other!" I took a deep breath, trying to rein in the anger, trying to channel the empathy Professor Davies talked about, the empathy Woody Guthrie sang about, the empathy that felt like the only real weapon we had left. "I know you're scared. We all are." I looked around the room, at Rhys's confused face, at Mack's stony expression, at Gem's quiet fury, at Jessica's raw terror. "Look at me – I'm on a visa that could get yanked if I sneeze wrong near a cop. That yellow triangle on my student portal isn't just a suggestion. It's a threat. They *want* me scared. They *want* you scared." My voice grew passionate, fueled by my own precariousness and my fear for my friends. "But that's *why* we have to fight back! For the people who can't! For the people they're trying to erase! For each other! For the idea that maybe GLAMA doesn't have to be this way!"

"Fighting back could get us *all* erased, Leo!" Rhys argued, looking genuinely frightened now, finally grasping maybe a fraction of the stakes. "Or deported, in your case! Is that what you want?"

"What I *want*," I said, meeting his gaze steadily, trying to convey the urgency, the weight of it, "is to not live in fear. What I *want* is for this creeping bullshit, this tide of hate and control, to stop. And playing nice for Sterling, hoping he throws us a few scraps from his table while he dismantles everything around us, isn't going to make that happen." I looked around at them again, my bandmates, my found family, seeing the different kinds of fear and frustration warring on their faces. "Look," I conceded, the energy draining out of me slightly, replaced by a grim practicality born of too many sleepless nights staring at the ceiling. "Maybe we *have* to play 'Different Lenses' next round. Fine. We're locked in. It's too late to change it. But we don't play it safe. We play it loud. We play it angry. We put everything we're feeling – the fear, the rage, the confusion, the solidarity – into every single note. We make them *hear* the static, even if they don't understand the words." I paused, gathering my resolve, the next thought forming, dangerous but necessary. "And then? Then we write something undeniable. Something they *can't* ignore. Something they can't sanitize. Something like... like Gem's 'Patriot Games'." I knew she'd been working on it; I'd seen the furious scribbles in her notebook, felt the shift in her energy, the focus of her anger.

Gemini nodded slowly, her eyes dark with resolve. Rhys looked confused but intrigued by the idea of a new, potentially powerful song – maybe something technically challenging he could sink his teeth into. Jessica just looked terrified, wrapping her arms around herself as if physically holding herself together. Mack watched us all, her expression unreadable but her hands gripping her sticks tightly, knuckles white.

"But we need a plan," I said, the thought solidifying even as I spoke it, born from the cold fear churning in my own gut, the flashing yellow triangle on the student portal, the memory of cold concrete and zip ties, the knowledge of my own precarious position. This wasn't just abstract politics; this was my life, my future, on the line. "Not just for the next song, but for... after. If things go sideways. If we push too hard and they push back harder. If playing a song gets someone deported, or worse." I hesitated, the words feeling heavy, almost treasonous to the hopeful energy we tried to maintain, the reason I came to GLAMA in the first place. "I have family back in Canada. It's stable there. Safe. I have connections." I looked around at their faces, wanting them to understand the seriousness, the potential reality, the safety net I could offer that they, ironically, couldn't access themselves. "It's... it's an option." My voice dropped. "An escape route. If we need one."

The words hung in the air, heavy and real. The idea of fleeing, of needing an escape route from a damn *band competition*, suddenly made the stakes terrifyingly clear. This wasn't just about music anymore, not just about winning or losing or getting noticed. It was about survival. And maybe, just maybe, it was about fighting for something more than just ourselves, even if it meant risking everything, even if it meant running away to fight another day.

CHAPTER 8: GEMINI

Another two weeks dissolved into the GLAMA haze, each day feeling heavier, more charged, more precarious than the last. The notification confirming our advancement to the Freedom's Ring Quarterfinals popped up on the slick portal like a reward for good behavior we hadn't actually exhibited. The relief was fleeting, a tiny gasp of air before plunging back under the murky water. We were deeper in the machine now, the stakes higher, the scrutiny more intense. The cage, as I'd called it, felt less like a metaphor and more like a closing reality.

The city itself felt different, too. Tenser. Like a guitar string tightened almost to its breaking point. The fallout from the "Family Harmony Act" continued to ripple outwards, creating visible fissures in the social landscape. There were more protests downtown, smaller now, maybe, but angrier, more desperate. They were met with swifter, more brutal responses from GLAMA PD and the black-uniformed CPB agents who seemed to materialize out of nowhere, their movements coordinated, efficient, chillingly impersonal. SNN barely covered them, and when they did, it was all carefully framed footage of "violent agitators" clashing with "heroic officers maintaining order," interspersed with solemn pronouncements from city officials about "zero tolerance for unrest." Online, dissent was harder to find, scrubbed faster by algorithms likely designed by Sterling Tech, buried under an avalanche of manufactured outrage about trivial culture war bullshit or glowing puff pieces about Sterling's latest philanthropic venture (usually involving some new surveillance tech generously "donated" to schools or public transit). The signal-to-noise ratio was getting worse every day. Did they add more cameras, or was I just noticing them more? It felt like the city was holding its breath, waiting for the next blow to fall.

Even the mundane felt menacing. One morning, I went out to where I usually parked the Rustbucket – my ancient, jailbroken Sterling Model Wee! – only to find the charging cable slashed clean through, lying uselessly on the cracked pavement like a dead snake. Just random vandalism? Maybe. GLAMA had plenty of that. Or maybe someone didn't like the "This Machine Kills Fascists" sticker plastered on the bumper. Or maybe it was a message, a subtle warning, a way to keep me off balance, make me late, remind me of my vulnerability. Paranoia felt less like a symptom these days and more like a necessary survival tool. It meant taking the notoriously unreliable GLAMA Metro across town for practice and the soundcheck, adding another layer of stress and potential delay to an already fraught situation. Relying on public transit felt like another small surrender to the system I despised.

The Metro ride itself was an exercise in observation, a rolling cross-section of the city's anxieties. More people seemed to be sleeping rough on the station benches, their faces etched with exhaustion and despair. Fewer people made eye contact, heads buried in phones or staring blankly ahead. Outside a hardware store near the warehouse district stop, a crowd of men – mostly Latino, mostly older – gathered hopefully near the entrance at dawn, waiting for day labor gigs that probably wouldn't materialize for most of them. It was a sight that felt like a throwback to grainy Dust Bowl photographs, suddenly sharp and present and deeply wrong in this gleaming, futuristic metropolis. The safety net wasn't just torn; it felt like it had been deliberately shredded and set on fire by the people in charge, the ones living comfortably behind gated communities and Sterling Security patrols.

And yet, amidst the decay and the fear, small signs of defiance flickered like faulty wiring. I saw more graffiti questioning the official narrative – quick, angry slashes of paint asking *"Who Watches Sterling?"* or crude drawings mocking the Mayor's latest pronouncements. Rhys had been right about the online buzz too, however faint; scrolling through less mainstream forums (the kind you needed encrypted access for), I found threads dissecting our prelim performance of "Torn to Shreds." People were arguing about the lyrics, sharing bootleg audio clips. Some dismissed us as noise, others praised the energy, a few even seemed to *get* the critique about the system. It was a strange, unsettling mix – hope and dread churning together in my gut. Were we actually connecting with anyone? Or were we just providing more fodder for the endless online arguments that changed nothing?

Practice remained a tightrope walk over a pit of simmering resentment and fear. We hammered away at "Different Lenses," trying to polish the rough edges, tightening the transitions before the Quarterfinals. Musically, it was coming together, maybe the most complex, most interesting thing we'd attempted. Leo's trumpet lines for the bridge were sharp, almost painful, perfectly capturing the song's anxious core. Jessica's guitar work was intricate, precise, layered with spiky, dissonant textures that felt raw and honest, though she still seemed to retreat behind that wall of technicality whenever we took a break, rarely meeting my eye. Rhys, surprisingly, seemed to genuinely enjoy the song's rhythmic complexity, focusing intently on locking in with Mack's shifting beat, though I suspected he still interpreted the lyrics as generic relationship angst rather than systemic critique. I even caught him trying to mimic Leo's trumpet phrases on his guitar during a break, a flash of his underlying musicality that almost made me smile, if the air wasn't so thick with unspoken dread. And Mack... Mack held it all together, her drumming a relentless, steady pulse beneath the dissonance, a grounding force in the sonic chaos.

But the *feeling*... the feeling was still off. The easy camaraderie, the shared understanding that used to spark between us when we really locked in – it was mostly gone, replaced by wary caution and unspoken anxieties. Jessica jumped every time her phone buzzed. Leo's usual jokes fell flat. Rhys kept trying to talk about competition strategy, oblivious to the emotional minefield around him. We were a collection of musicians playing the same song, but it didn't always feel like we were a *band*. Especially not when the song ended and the silence rushed back in, filled with everything we weren't saying, everything we were too scared or too angry or too confused to articulate.

Getting into the Sterling Grand Auditorium for the Quarterfinal soundcheck was its own special kind of hell. Thanks to the slashed charger cable and the Metro deciding to spontaneously experience "signal problems" (a common occurrence when protests were scheduled downtown), I was running late, arriving flustered and sweating. The Sterling Security guard at the artist entrance, a burly guy with mirrored sunglasses and an expression like carved granite, took an suspiciously long time examining my laminated competitor badge, his thumb hovering over his tablet.

"Jones, Gemini," he grunted, his voice flat, devoid of inflection. He tapped aggressively on his Sterling™ tablet. "Doesn't look like you're on the approved access list for this time slot."

My heart hammered. "I am," I insisted, trying to keep my voice steady, trying not to sound defensive, acutely aware of the sleek SNN camera mounted above the doorway, its lens like a black, unblinking eye. "Jessica's Jones. Quarterfinalist soundcheck scheduled for 3 PM. Check again."

He scrolled slowly, deliberately, his thumb swiping across the screen with agonizing slowness, making a show of it. "Hmm. System's slow today. Lots of traffic." He looked me up and down then, his gaze lingering just a little too long on my ripped jeans, my worn-out band shirt, my skin color. Making me feel out of place, unwelcome. Was this racism? Standard bureaucratic incompetence amplified by petty power-tripping? Or something more targeted, a deliberate hassle orchestrated from higher up?

In GLAMA these days, it was getting harder and harder to tell the difference. Paranoia felt like rational self-preservation. Finally, after what felt like an eternity measured in heartbeats, he grunted again. "Fine. Go ahead. But stay in the designated artist areas. Don't wander." He buzzed me through the heavy glass door without making eye contact, dismissing me.

I hurried through the now-familiar beige, aggressively air-conditioned hallways, my bass case banging against my leg, arriving breathless at the designated conference room just as the band was being called into *another* mandatory pre-performance meeting. This wasn't the usual stage manager; this was someone higher up, a woman in a sharp, impeccably tailored Sterling Corp blazer, platinum blonde hair pulled back in a severe bun, an unnervingly pleasant smile fixed on her face, and eyes like chips of ice. She radiated expensive efficiency and barely concealed contempt.

"Just a quick check-in, bands," she announced, her voice crisp and amplified slightly by the room's acoustics, cutting through the nervous chatter. "Hope everyone's feeling ready to showcase their talent for GLAMA!" Her eyes swept the room, lingering for a fraction of a second longer on the punk bands, the ones with the ripped clothes and defiant attitudes, including us. "As you know, Freedom's Ring is dedicated to celebrating positive community values and artistic excellence." She consulted her tablet, the Sterling logo gleaming on the back. "In light of recent events, and ensuring a harmonious broadcast experience for our SNN viewers nationwide, we're implementing a slight policy adjustment for the Quarterfinals and beyond." She looked up, her smile tightening almost imperceptibly. "We'll now require lyric sheets submitted electronically for pre-approval for any original songs performed from this round forward. Just a formality, of course," she added quickly, anticipating the murmurs of protest already starting, "to ensure compliance with broadcast standards and prevent any... misunderstandings due to ambiguous or potentially offensive language." She smiled again, the expression not reaching her cold eyes. "Wouldn't want any language deemed potentially inflammatory or disruptive to detract from the spirit of unity we're fostering here, would we?"

A cold silence fell over the room. Lyric pre-approval. It was blatant censorship, dressed up in corporate doublespeak about "harmony" and "broadcast standards." My hand tightened on my bass case until my knuckles turned white. So much for fighting them on their own turf; they were already dictating the terms of engagement, demanding we hand over our weapons – our words – for inspection and potential confiscation before the battle even started. I saw some of the other bands exchange uneasy glances. The guys from Static Bloom, an older rock band who'd clearly sanded off their edges to fit in, just nodded along, looking relieved. Heartwood, the folk group whose traditional songs were now dripping with nationalist sentiment, beamed approvingly.

"What constitutes 'inflammatory' or 'disruptive'?" someone from another punk band – a girl with bright green hair and piercings – asked, her voice sharp with challenge.

The woman's smile didn't waver. It was terrifyingly practiced. "That will be determined by Sterling Media's Standards & Practices department on a case-by-case basis, ensuring alignment with community values and advertiser sensitivities. Just submit the lyrics through the portal at least one hour prior to your performance time. Simple." She clapped her hands together briskly, a sharp, dismissive sound. "Alright! Break a leg, everyone! Make GLAMA proud!"

Back in our designated backstage waiting area (another beige box, this one smelling faintly of stale popcorn), the mood was mutinous. "Lyric approval? Are you fucking kidding me?" Leo paced back and forth in the cramped space, agitated, running a hand through his already messy hair. "This is straight-up censorship! Bullshit!"

"Told you," I muttered, sinking onto a plastic chair and pulling out my notebook, needing to sketch the ice-eyed woman in the blazer, capture the coldness in her smile. "The cage door. It's closing."

"So what do we do?" Jessica asked, her voice trembling slightly. She was hugging herself, looking pale. "We already submitted 'Different Lenses' as our song title. Do we have to send the lyrics now? What if they don't approve them?"

"Guess so," Mack said grimly, already tapping away on her phone, navigating the competitor portal. "New requirement just popped up. Deadline is one hour before performance time." She looked up, her expression unreadable. "Better get typing, Gem."

"Great," I sighed, pulling out the crumpled page with the lyrics. "Guess they get to read my questionable poetry after all." At least "Different Lenses," while anxious and critical, wasn't overtly calling for revolution. Its critique was buried in metaphor, in the feeling. It might just slip under their radar. Unlike the lyrics for "Patriot Games" currently burning a hole in my other notebook, hidden deep in my backpack. Those words felt like contraband now.

The Quarterfinal performance itself felt like walking a tightrope over a pool of sharks, in lead boots. The theater was slightly more full this time, the pressure higher, the air colder. We played "Different Lenses." I tried to channel all the accumulated frustration – the slashed charger cable, the security hassle, the lyric submission, the chilling news about the Harmony Act, the suffocating weight of the competition itself – into the performance. The song's nervous energy felt amplified by our own frayed nerves, the dissonant chords sharper, the rhythm more frantic, bordering on chaotic but held together by Mack's relentless precision.

I forced myself to look out at the audience this time, past the blinding stage lights. Saw the scattering of familiar faces from the punk scene near the back, looking wary but supportive. Saw the nervous parents. Saw the bored industry scouts. Saw the impassive rows of Sterling executives in the front, their faces like identical masks. I sang the words directly at them, trying to inject every ounce of anxiety and anger I felt. *You hear comfort, I hear lies / Behind those calculated eyes...*

The band locked in behind me, fueled by a shared sense of being under siege. Jessica's playing was sharp, angular, her usual fluidity replaced by a controlled, brittle tension that perfectly matched the song's fractured mood. Leo's trumpet stabs felt like warning sirens cutting through the static. Even Rhys seemed to feed off the strange energy, his rhythm guitar tighter, more focused than usual, his usual stage-fright replaced by a kind of fierce concentration. Maybe he was finally feeling some of the pressure, the sense that this wasn't just a game.

For four minutes, we were locked in, creating something raw and unsettling and maybe even powerful on that sterile, corporate stage. When we finished, the reaction was... strange. Definitely not the confused politeness of the prelims. There was actual applause, louder this time, more sustained, especially from the back of the room. But also pockets of stony silence, particularly from the front rows where the Sterling execs sat, unmoving. I saw a few people leaning forward during the performance, looking intrigued, maybe even disturbed. Had we connected? Had the message somehow cut through the noise, despite the censors, despite the venue? Or had we just confused them more? The judges scribbled furiously on their tablets, their faces unreadable masks. The woman with the severe glasses still looked unimpressed, maybe even annoyed.

As we cleared the stage, feeling drained and uncertain, adrift in the post-performance adrenaline crash, Rick Anderson, the smarmy producer, materialized again, gliding towards Jessica with that predatory smile. This time, however, he didn't just stop at her. He beckoned me over too, his eyes flicking between us. My stomach clenched. This couldn't be good.

"Jessica, Gemini," he began, his voice smooth as ever, though his eyes seemed colder, harder than before. "Another... energetic performance. Very... atmospheric." He paused, letting the word hang there, dripping with faint condescension. "Technically strong, of course. Your musicianship is undeniable." Another pause. "But the overall message... a little unclear, wouldn't you say? A bit downbeat for Freedom's Ring. Remember what we talked about? Unity. Positivity. Connecting with the heartland." He gestured vaguely, as if 'the heartland' was a focus group demographic on his tablet.

Before I could retort that maybe the heartland was feeling pretty downbeat too, he continued, his gaze flicking between us, assessing. "We were thinking, for the next round – assuming you advance, of course," he added, the implication clear, "perhaps something more... universally appealing? We have some excellent songwriters on staff, Grammy winners actually, who could collaborate, help you craft something with real broadcast potential. Something that truly captures the spirit of resilience and optimism that defines GLAMA." He gestured towards the stage manager, who obediently held up a tablet displaying what looked like... outfit sketches? Shiny fabrics, coordinated colors, maybe even some tasteful flag motifs. My stomach churned. "And visually," Anderson went on, oblivious to my internal gag reflex, "we need to think about cohesion. That punk look is... specific. Niche. We have some wonderful stylists contracted, top industry people, they could really help you craft a look that resonates better with the wider SNN audience. Maybe something coordinated? Brighter colors? More... aspirational?"

Stylists. Songwriters. Aspirational outfits. My blood ran cold. This wasn't just suggestion anymore; this was assimilation disguised as helpful advice. They wanted to gut us, sand us down, paint us beige, turn us into another compliant product for Sterling's machine, another smiling face for the propaganda posters.

"We pick our own songs," I said, my voice dangerously quiet, my hands clenched into fists at my sides. "And we wear our own clothes."

Anderson's smile tightened almost imperceptibly at the edges, a flicker of annoyance crossing his smooth features before being instantly suppressed. "Of course, of course," he said, his voice dripping with false sincerity. "Artistic integrity is paramount. We respect that." He sounded like he was reading from a script memorized in countless corporate seminars. "These are just suggestions. Resources available to help you reach your full potential. Maximize your impact. We just want you to succeed." He gave another blinding smile that didn't reach his eyes, cold and calculating. "We'll be in touch about the results. Keep up the good work." He turned and walked away, leaving the suggestion hanging in the air like a threat, heavy and suffocating.

Back in the beige holding room, the air crackled with unspoken fury and fear. "Stylists?" Leo spat, incredulous, pacing the small space. "Songwriters? They want to turn us into fucking Synthēsis? Did you see those silver jumpsuits?"

"And 'universally appealing' songs?" I added, feeling sick to my stomach. "He means songs with no teeth, no message. Songs that won't offend Sterling's advertisers or question the official narrative."

Rhys looked conflicted, torn between his desire for success and his dawning awareness that maybe this wasn't the straightforward opportunity he'd hoped for. "Well... maybe coordinated outfits wouldn't be so bad?" he offered weakly, fiddling with his guitar strap. "Iron Eagle looks pretty put-together..."

"Rhys!" Leo and I snapped at the same time, Leo adding a string of frustrated French curses under his breath.

Just then, Mack's phone buzzed insistently in her pocket. She pulled it out, glanced at the screen, her usual impassive expression hardening into something grim, alert. She answered, listened for a moment, her eyes narrowing almost imperceptibly, then ended the call abruptly with a quiet, "Copy that."

"What is it?" Jessica asked, her voice barely a whisper. She looked like she was about to shatter.

Mack looked up, her gaze sweeping over us, pausing for a fraction of a second on Leo, then settling finally on Jessica, her expression unreadable but radiating bad news. "That was Sal," she said, her voice flat, devoid of emotion, which somehow made it even more chilling. "He just got released. CPB picked him up this afternoon. Held him for six hours."

My blood turned to ice. The air left my lungs. "Sal? Why? What happened?"

Mack's eyes were hard, direct. "They were asking about 'dissident activity' at the club," she reported, her voice clipped, precise. "Asking about benefit shows he hosted last year. Asking specifically... about us. About Jessica's Jones. Wanted names. Schedules. What kind of 'message' we were promoting."

The room went absolutely silent. The producer's veiled threats, the lyric checks, the suggestion about stylists, the slashed charging cable, Leo's visa status warning – it all snapped into sharp, terrifying focus. This wasn't just about controlling the message on a TV show anymore. This was real-world intimidation. This was the state apparatus targeting not just us, but people associated with us. This was about making examples. The cage door wasn't just creaking now. It felt like it was slamming shut, locking us inside with the machine, and the machine had teeth.

CHAPTER 9:
JESSICA LAMAS

The waiting was the worst part. Always was. After our Quarterfinal performance of "Different Lenses," after Rick Anderson's chillingly polite "suggestions" that felt more like directives, after Mack's bombshell news about Sal being picked up by the CPB, we were relegated back to the beige backstage holding room, adrift in a sea of nervous energy and unspoken fear. The air tasted stale, recycled, thick with the smell of old carpet and too many anxious bodies crammed into one space. The results wouldn't be announced until all the bands had played, maybe hours from now. Hours trapped together in this sterile box, the silence punctuated only by the aggressive hum of the fluorescent lights overhead and the frantic tapping of Leo's foot against the cheap linoleum floor. Outside these soundproofed walls, the city – our city – felt like it was fraying at the seams, tearing itself apart while we sat here waiting for judgment from the very people pulling the strings.

I paced the length of the small room – maybe ten steps one way, ten steps back – too agitated to sit, too anxious to talk. My fingers kept finding the strings of my Les Paul, picking out nervous, disjointed patterns, needing the familiar feel of the smooth wood and cool metal under my fingertips, a physical anchor in the swirling chaos of my thoughts. Sal. Picked up. Questioned about *us*. About *dissidents*. The word itself felt dangerous, radioactive. Sal, who always smelled faintly of stale beer and cigarettes, who let us play even when we drew maybe ten people, who represented the gritty, independent heart of the punk scene we were supposedly part of – he was vulnerable. And if *he* was vulnerable, despite being a citizen, a business owner, what did that mean for us? For Leo, with that flashing yellow warning triangle next to his visa status on the student portal? For me, now that Rick Anderson, Sterling's slick mouthpiece, had made it terrifyingly clear they knew exactly who my father was, dropping his name like a casual threat? *Families appreciate stability... Wouldn't want any unnecessary static...* The words echoed in my head, no longer just a vague warning but a direct, chilling implication. Play nice, or the stability your family enjoys might just... disappear. The safety net I'd always taken for granted, woven from my parents' success and connections, suddenly felt thin and frayed, maybe even like a trap itself. A line from one of Gemini's songs, "Torn to Shreds," snagged in my mind – "The safety net is torn to shreds..." I'd always thought of it as an abstract thing, something happening to other people, something Gemini was angry about *for* them. But now, with Anderson's words, with Sal... it felt like my own net was ripping, and the same hands were holding the knife. It wasn't just a song anymore; it was a cold, hard knot of fear in my own stomach.

Gemini sat hunched in a corner, sketchbook open on her lap but pen still, staring blankly at the page. Her usual sharp focus seemed blurred, replaced by something that looked like bone-deep exhaustion, or maybe despair. The weight of the world always seemed to rest heavier on her shoulders. Leo leaned against the wall near the door, scrolling furiously through his phone, his face grim, occasionally muttering curses in French under his breath as he searched encrypted news feeds for updates on the situation outside. Rhys was attempting small talk with a couple of guys from another band – a bland indie-pop outfit called 'The Sunny Disposition' or something equally ironic – trying to act normal, trying to network, probably, talking about gear and exposure, but even his forced cheerfulness seemed strained around the edges, his eyes darting nervously towards the door. And Mack sat on an overturned equipment case, methodically cleaning her already spotless drum hardware with a soft cloth, her movements precise, economical, a small island of calm in the swirling chaos, though the tightness around her eyes, the almost imperceptible tension in her jaw, betrayed the strain. She saw everything, missed nothing. What was she thinking? Did she regret getting involved with us?

My phone buzzed, startling me. A text from Mom: *Saw you advanced online! Wonderful news, sweetie! Your father is so proud. Call us when you can! Stay safe!* Stay safe. Easy for them to say from their secure house up in the hills, behind the gates and the Sterling Security™ patrols. Did they have any idea what was really happening down here? Did they understand the fear that coiled in my stomach every time I thought about Anderson's veiled threat? I felt a familiar surge of resentment, quickly followed by a wave of guilt. They loved me, I knew they did, in their own way. They just didn't understand. They didn't see the cracks Gemini pointed out, didn't feel the chill Leo carried with him like a second skin. They lived in the world Sterling presented on SNN – orderly, prosperous, safe, as long as you followed the rules and didn't look too closely at who got crushed underfoot to maintain that order. They believed in the system because the system had always worked for them.

Just then, a commotion erupted from the larger common area outside our holding room, where a big SNN screen usually showed bland promotional loops for Sterling Corp ventures or sanitized clips from previous competition rounds. Shouts, gasps, the sound of running feet in the hallway. Leo was closest to the door; he poked his head out cautiously, then quickly pulled back, his face pale, eyes wide.

"What is it?" I asked, my heart starting to pound against my ribs like a frantic drumbeat.

"Trouble," Leo breathed, his voice strained. "Big trouble. Sterling was doing a live press conference outside the Auditorium... some bullshit about 'celebrating GLAMA's resilience' during the competition... and someone threw something, I think it exploded... then... shit. They're firing into the crowd!"

We crowded towards the doorway, peering out at the screen just as the feed dissolved into chaos. The SNN camera, clearly handheld now, spun wildly. We saw jerky footage – Sterling standing at a podium moments before, flanked by his usual phalanx of imposing Sterling Security guards in their sharp grey uniforms, then a sudden movement from the edge of the frame, something dark arcing through the air towards the stage, a bright flash near the podium – like a firecracker, almost, small and quick – followed by Sterling flinching back instinctively. His security detail instantly drew weapons, forming a human shield around him, shoving him towards the backstage entrance. Then shouting, screaming from the crowd, the camera swinging wildly, catching terrifying glimpses of guards aiming weapons *outwards*, muzzle flashes, people falling, sheer panic erupting... and then the feed abruptly cut. Replaced instantly by the calm, smiling face of an SNN anchor back in the pristine studio.

"We seem to be experiencing technical difficulties with our live feed from the Sterling Grand Auditorium," the anchor said smoothly, her expression utterly untroubled, not a hair out of place. "We'll return to that story as soon as possible. Meanwhile, in financial news, Sterling Consolidated shares reached an all-time high today following the announcement of their new 'Secure City' initiative – a landmark 99-year contract awarded to their Sterling Security division to provide comprehensive security services and operational support for GLAMA PD, all under the direct oversight of the Citizen Protection Bureau. A bold step for a safer GLAMA, analysts are saying."

My blood ran cold. The casual brutality, the instant media sanitization... it was horrifying.

The door to our holding room burst open before we could even process what we'd seen. The ice-eyed woman in the Sterling Corp blazer stood there, flanked by two grim-faced Sterling Security guards, their hands resting ominously near the sidearms holstered on their belts. Her professional smile was gone, replaced by a tight, hard line, her eyes scanning the room with cold authority.

"Attention, all performers and staff," she announced, her voice sharp, clipped, cutting through the sudden, terrified silence in the room. "Due to an ongoing security incident outside the venue, the GLAMA Police Department, in coordination with the Citizen Protection Bureau, has declared a city-wide state of emergency and implemented martial law protocols, effective immediately."

Martial law? The words hung in the air, heavy, unbelievable. My mind struggled to grasp the implications. Curfews were one thing, checkpoints another, but *martial law*? Troops on the streets? Suspended rights? It felt like something from a history book, not something happening *now, here*.

"For your own safety," the woman continued, her eyes sweeping the room again, devoid of any empathy or reassurance, "this facility is now under lockdown. No one is permitted to enter or leave until the all-clear is given by CPB command. Transportation services are suspended city-wide. Communication networks may be experiencing disruptions." Her gaze lingered on us, on the other bands with their ripped shirts and defiant attitudes. "Please remain calm and await further instructions. The competition schedule will proceed as planned within the venue. Your cooperation is expected." The implication was clear: the show must go on, even if the city outside was burning. She turned on her heel and left, the security guards taking up positions outside the door, their faces impassive, their presence a tangible threat.

Trapped. We were literally trapped inside the Sterling Grand Auditorium while martial law descended on the city outside. Panic clawed at my throat, cold and sharp. My parents. Were they okay? What was happening out there? Were people really getting shot?

"My God," Rhys whispered, his face white as bleached bone.

"Martial law? What does that even mean?"

Leo swore violently in French again, pacing the small room like a caged animal, running agitated hands through his hair. "They just opened fire! Did they even see who threw that thing? How many innocent people were just shot out there because of some damn firecracker? And SNN just cuts away like nothing happened!"

Gemini was silent, her face grim, knuckles white where she gripped her sketchbook as if it were a life raft. Mack stood near the door, her stance subtly shifted into something watchful, assessing the guards outside, her hand resting almost imperceptibly near the heavy multi-tool clipped to her belt.

My first instinct, overwhelming and desperate, was to call my parents. I fumbled for my phone, my fingers clumsy, but the signal bars were gone. Blank. "Network disruptions," the woman had said. Convenient. Of course, the Sterling™ tablets provided in the room for accessing the competition portal – the ones connected to *their* secure network – still worked perfectly. I grabbed one, my hands shaking, heart pounding, and initiated a video call, praying they were home, praying they were safe.

Mom answered almost immediately, her face appearing on the small screen, pale and etched with worry. Dad hovered anxiously behind her, his usual confident demeanor replaced by uncertainty. "Jessica! Mija! Are you alright? We saw the news... it looked awful! What happened?" Mom's voice was high-pitched with anxiety. "I'm okay, Mom. I'm fine," I lied, trying to keep my voice steady, trying to project a calm I didn't feel. "We're inside the auditorium. They've locked it down. We can't leave." "Locked down? Martial law?" Dad sounded incredulous, pushing closer to the screen, peering at me. "That seems... excessive for a protest, or whatever that was." Even he couldn't quite swallow the SNN spin this time, the reality too stark. "They said it's for our safety," I repeated the official line, the words tasting like ash in my mouth. "They're continuing the competition inside." "Well, that's good, I suppose," Mom said, clearly trying to find a positive angle, grasping for normalcy. "At least you're safe in there. Don't worry about us, we're fine, just staying inside. You just stay put and do what they tell you. Focus on your performance, sweetie. Make us proud." "Yeah, Jess," Dad added, trying for reassurance, falling back on familiar platitudes. "Just keep your head down, don't get involved in any trouble. This will all blow over soon. Sterling knows how to handle these things, maintain order." Keep my head down. Don't get involved. Sterling knows how to handle things. Their words, meant to be comforting, felt like another set of bars closing around me. But it wasn't some abstract "system" they were trusting. It was *Sterling*. The man whose executive, Rick Anderson, had looked me in the eye and subtly threatened my family. The man whose media empire was likely painting the band as villains even now. My parents didn't understand; they couldn't. They saw Sterling as the guarantor of order, the one who would make things safe. I knew, with a chilling certainty that settled deep in my bones, that Sterling *was* the danger. He wasn't the solution; he was the architect of the fear that was now gripping my family, even if they couldn't see his hand directly. The disconnect felt wider, deeper than ever. "Okay, Mom. Okay, Dad," I managed, my throat tight. "I... I have to go. Soundcheck soon." I ended the call quickly before they could see the tears welling up, before my carefully constructed composure shattered completely.

The hours crawled by in a haze of fear, uncertainty, and stale, recycled air. We got word through the portal – almost anticlimactically, amidst the chaos – that we *had* advanced to the Semi-Finals. The notification landed with a thud, feeling less like a victory and more like a sentence. Now we *had* to perform again, tomorrow night, trapped in this building, under martial law, with the stakes feeling impossibly, terrifyingly high.

The inevitable argument about the Semi-Final song started almost immediately, fueled by fear, adrenaline, and the claustrophobia of the lockdown. We huddled together on the floor, the pretense of normalcy gone.

"It has to be 'Patriot Games'," Gemini insisted, her voice low but intense, vibrating with suppressed fury. We'd all heard the song, worked on it even, back in the garage after the "Family Harmony Act" news hit. It was raw, furious, a Molotov cocktail aimed straight at Sterling, at the competition, at the whole damn system, disguised as a critique of blind nationalism. We'd shelved it almost immediately, agreeing – even me, reluctantly – that it was too dangerous, too confrontational for Freedom's Ring. But now... "Now more than ever," Gemini continued, her eyes burning with a dark fire I hadn't seen before. "Look what's happening outside! People getting shot for throwing a bottle rocket? Martial law declared over *that*? We can't play something safe now. We can't play 'Free to Be'. It's too... tame. It doesn't say enough."

"Doesn't say enough?" I cried, stung, the words hitting that raw nerve exposed by the song itself, the song that felt like *our* secret. "'Free to Be' is about wanting something real! It *does* say something!" Even as I said it, I knew she meant politically, but the personal meaning, the one I couldn't voice, felt dismissed, trivialized in the face of martial law. "Gem, we can't play 'Patriot Games'! We *know* that song is too hot! It's practically calling for revolution! After what Anderson said? After Sal getting picked up? After *this*?" I gestured wildly at the tablet still showing the SNN logo, the only connection to the outside world, now probably spewing lies about the "terrorist attack" on Sterling. "They'll arrest us on stage! Or worse! Think about my family! Think about what they could do!" The fear was a physical thing now, cold and tight in my chest, making it hard to breathe.

"What about *our* family?" Leo cut in, his voice raw with anger and his own fear. "What about the people getting shot outside? What about the rights they just stripped away? Isn't that worth fighting for? Winning isn't the point, remember?" He threw Gemini's earlier words back like a challenge, his eyes flashing.

"Winning keeps us *safe*!" Rhys argued, siding with me, but for different reasons, his eyes wide with a fear that was less about principles and more about immediate, personal consequences. "Winning gets us exposure! 'Free to Be' is catchy, people liked it at the screening! It's the smart choice! 'Patriot Games' – yeah, it has a killer riff," he conceded, appealing to my musical side, "I love playing it, but it's *career suicide*! We all agreed it was too much before this lockdown even happened!"

"Maybe some things are more important than a career, Rhys!" Gemini snapped back, her patience finally fraying completely.

"Like what? Getting disappeared?" I shot back, the fear making my voice shake, tears threatening again. "Is that what you want, Gem? For us? For Leo? For *me*?"

Gemini looked at me then, really looked at me, and her expression softened slightly, the anger replaced by something else, something pained, conflicted. "No, Jess," she said, her voice quieter now, but still intense, vibrating with conviction. "That's not what I want. I know you're scared. I am too." She took a deep, ragged breath, running a hand over her short, blue mohawk. "But playing safe, pretending none of this is happening... pretending *we* aren't happening..." Her voice dropped lower, charged with an emotion that went beyond politics. "That feels like disappearing too, in a different way. It feels like letting them win, letting them define us, letting them decide what we're allowed to be, who we're allowed to love." She gestured around the sterile room, at the Sterling logos everywhere. "This whole competition, this whole *city*... it's built on lies, on making people afraid to be real, afraid to connect authentically. We have this one chance, on their stage, with their cameras rolling... don't we have to use it? Don't we have to be authentic, even if it's dangerous? Isn't that the whole point? Isn't that what being free to be is *really* about? Being free to feel something real, even if it's scary? *Like how I feel about you, Jess!*"

The words tumbled out, louder than she intended, raw and unpremeditated. She stopped instantly, her eyes widening in horror at what she'd just said, her hand flying up too late to cover her mouth. The air crackled, charged with the weight of the unspoken finally, irrevocably, spoken.

Silence. Thick, suffocating silence filled the beige room. My heart stopped, then started again with a painful, violent lurch against my ribs. She'd said it. Out loud. In front of everyone. The thing I knew, the thing I felt pulsing between us like a dangerous, high-voltage current, the thing I was terrified to name, especially now, especially after the new law made it a crime, made *us* a potential crime. I couldn't breathe. My face felt hot, then cold, then hot again. I saw Rhys recoil almost imperceptibly, his eyes darting between me and Gemini, a look of confusion quickly replaced by something else – distaste? Discomfort? Judgment? – flickering across his face before he looked away, suddenly fascinated by his own expensive sneakers. Leo looked shocked for a second, his mouth slightly open, then his expression softened into something like sad understanding, a quick, pained glance towards me that acknowledged the impossible weight just dropped in my lap. Mack just watched me, her gaze steady, unreadable as ever, but maybe with a hint of… something? Sympathy? Warning? A silent question: *What now?*

And me? I felt like the floor had dropped out from under me. Exposed. Terrified. My carefully constructed walls – the good daughter, the serious musician, the straight girl – crumbled in an instant, leaving me raw and defenseless. And maybe, underneath the terror, underneath the panic of being seen, of being named in this dangerous new world, a tiny, treacherous spark of… something else flickered. Relief? Hope? Validation? The sheer, overwhelming rightness of it, despite everything? I couldn't process it. Not here. Not now. All I could feel was the raw, overwhelming weight of the danger, for both of us, multiplied tenfold by the words hanging in the air.

Just then, the door opened again. The polo-shirt woman stood there, clipboard in hand, utterly oblivious to the emotional wreckage inside the room, her professional smile firmly, brightly in place. "Jessica's Jones?" she chirped, her voice jarringly cheerful.

"Congratulations on advancing to the Semi-Finals! Wardrobe needs your measurements immediately!"

The cage door slammed shut, locking us all inside together, with nowhere left to hide.

CHAPTER 10:
MACKENZIE CALVERT

The air in the beige holding room crackled, thick with the fallout from Gemini's accidental detonation. Like the ozone smell after a lightning strike, but instead of ozone, it was pure, uncut emotional shrapnel. Words hung there, heavy, dangerous: Like how I feel about you, Jess! Said too loud, too raw, in the middle of an already volatile argument about song choices and survival. A critical error in judgment, exposing a flank right when the enemy was probing for weaknesses.

My gaze swept the room, assessing the immediate damage, cataloging reactions like potential threats on a battlefield map. Jessica: Target acquired, direct hit. Looked like she'd been struck by lightning – pale, trembling, eyes wide with a mixture of terror and something else I couldn't quite parse. Shock, definitely. But deeper, too. Like seeing a ghost or recognizing a truth she'd spent her whole life trying not to see. Vulnerable. Compromised. Rhys: Collateral damage, but reacting predictably. Recoiled physically, face flushing then paling, eyes darting anywhere but at Gemini or Jessica. Radiating pure, uncomfortable awkwardness mixed with a visible distaste, probably fueled by whatever homophobic bullshit SNN and his privileged upbringing fed him daily. A weak link, susceptible to external influence. Leo: Momentarily stunned, processing the blast radius, then his expression shifted to a kind of weary sympathy, mostly directed at Jessica. He knew the score, probably better than anyone besides me and Gem. He understood the danger, the added layer of risk this revelation piled onto their already precarious situation.

And Gemini... Gemini looked utterly mortified. Her hand was still clamped over her mouth, as if she could physically shove the words back in. Her eyes, usually sharp and analytical, were wide with disbelief at her own tactical blunder. The fierce conviction from moments before had evaporated, replaced by a raw vulnerability and immediate, palpable regret. She wouldn't meet Jessica's shocked gaze. Tactical error, major breach of operational security, revealing a critical vulnerability under fire. Not like her. Usually, she had better fire discipline than this. The pressure, the lockdown, the constant threat assessment – it was getting to everyone, fraying nerves, causing mistakes.

Then the door opened, shattering the fragile, charged silence like a poorly timed mortar round. The polo-shirt woman, Ms. Corporate Efficiency herself, chirped about the Semi-Finals and wardrobe measurements, completely oblivious, or maybe just deliberately ignoring, the emotional carnage inside the room. Perfect timing. Saved by the machine we were supposedly fighting. The irony was thick enough to choke on. Another reminder that our internal struggles, our messy human feelings, were completely irrelevant to the smooth functioning of Sterling's entertainment-propaganda complex.

The interruption broke the spell, but the tension remained, a low-frequency hum beneath the surface, vibrating through the cheap carpet. Nobody addressed what Gemini had said. Nobody could. Not here, not now, trapped in this beige box under lockdown, with Sterling Security guards – essentially private military contractors in slightly less intimidating uniforms – posted just outside the door. We retreated into ourselves, the earlier arguments about song choice momentarily forgotten, overshadowed by this new, far more dangerous revelation. Jessica sank onto a plastic chair, wrapping her arms around herself as if physically holding herself together, staring blankly at the floor, lost in whatever internal storm had just been unleashed. Gemini retreated to the furthest corner, turning her back to us, ostensibly checking her bass strings again, but I could see the rigid set of her shoulders, the slight tremor in her hands. She was regrouping, assessing her error, probably hating herself for it. Leo started pacing again, four steps one way, four steps back, restless energy radiating off him like heat shimmer. Rhys busied himself with his phone, pretending intense interest in something, anything, else, desperate to avoid the emotional fallout zone. Standard avoidance behavior.

The wardrobe people came eventually, two assistants armed with tape measures and tablets, their forced cheerfulness grating like sand in gears. They fussed over measurements, chattering about "brand synergy" and "visual narratives" and "connecting with the key demographics." Empty corporate jargon designed to make manipulation sound like opportunity. I endured it stoically, giving them nothing but flat responses and minimal cooperation. They tried to suggest something "a little softer" for my look, maybe something "more approachable." I just stared back, holding their gaze without blinking, until they faltered and retreated with nervous smiles. Some battles weren't worth the energy; a direct refusal was more efficient than arguing aesthetics with programmed drones.

Later, after the wardrobe vultures left, leaving behind the rack of hideous, unwanted costumes like a monument to corporate cluelessness, the conversation inevitably, awkwardly, circled back to the Semi-Final setlist. We were scheduled to play tomorrow night. The lockdown was still in effect, the official portal feeding us sanitized updates about the "security situation" outside – escalating unrest contained by decisive CPB action, peaceful assembly zones designated (and likely surrounded), essential services maintained (for those who could afford them). The usual Sterling-approved narrative. We needed a song. And we needed it now.

The argument resumed with a vengeance, the earlier tension now supercharged by Gemini's confession and the claustrophobia of the lockdown. It was like watching a fire reignite in a munitions dump.

"It *has* to be 'Patriot Games'," Gemini insisted, her voice low but vibrating with a desperate intensity. She'd recovered some of her fire, but it was brittle now, edged with something close to recklessness. "After what happened out there? After the lockdown? We can't play nice. We can't play 'Free to Be'. It's... it's not enough. It doesn't say what needs to be said."

Jessica, who had been a ghost since Gemini's outburst, flinched as if struck. "Not enough?" she whispered, her voice trembling, eyes wide and wounded. "Gem, that song... it means..." She trailed off, unable to articulate it, looking utterly betrayed.

"I know what it means, Jess," Gemini said, her voice softening for a fraction of a second, a flicker of pain in her own eyes before hardening again. "But this is bigger than that now. This is about them trying to shut us down, shut everyone down. 'Patriot Games' is the only answer."

"The answer is to get us all arrested?" Rhys practically shrieked, his voice cracking. He jumped up from where he'd been moodily scrolling on his phone. "Are you insane, Gemini? 'Patriot Games' is a suicide mission! We all agreed! And after what you just... what you said about 'Free to Be'..." He gestured vaguely, his face flushing a dark red, a mixture of anger and profound discomfort. "That song's not even... it's not *right* anymore! It's... it's messed up! We should play something straightforward, something that won't get us thrown in a CPB van!" His earlier desire for fame seemed to have been completely eclipsed by raw fear and a new, ugly layer of judgment. The regime's propaganda about the "Family Harmony Act," about "traditional values," had clearly found fertile ground in his insecurity and his desire to conform.

"So we just roll over?" Leo shot back, his fists clenched. "We let Sterling and his goons dictate what's 'right'? Gemini's right, we need to hit them hard! And Jess," he said, his voice softening slightly as he turned to her, "Gemini also said 'winning isn't the point,' remember? Maybe this is one of those times." He was echoing Gemini's earlier words, but the context felt heavier now, the stakes lethally real.

"Winning keeps us *safe!*" Jessica cried, her voice raw with terror, tears finally spilling over, tracing clean paths through the dust on her cheeks. "Winning gets us out of here! 'Free to Be' is the song they know, the one they might let us play without... without consequences! Please, Gem, please! Think about my family! Think about what Anderson said! They can *hurt* them!" The producer's veiled threat had clearly landed, a seed of fear now blooming into full-blown panic.

The room felt like a pressure cooker. Jessica pleading for safety, her fear a tangible thing. Gemini, driven by a desperate need to fight back, to make a statement, even if it was self-destructive. Leo, caught between his revolutionary ideals and his concern for his friends. And Rhys, now openly hostile, his fear curdling into something uglier, parroting the regime's talking points.

Gemini looked from Jessica's tear-streaked face to Leo's defiant one, then to Rhys's disgusted sneer. The fire in her seemed to waver, then dim. She took a deep, shuddering breath. "Fine," she said, the word choked, heavy with defeat. "We play 'Free to Be'." Her voice was flat, devoid of all emotion. She wouldn't look at any of us. It was a surrender, I knew, not of principle, but to protect Jessica, to de-escalate the immediate, explosive conflict. A tactical retreat, but the cost was etched on her face.

The silence that followed was thick with unspoken resentments and the bitter taste of compromise. Rhys let out a shaky breath, looking relieved and slightly smug. Leo just shook his head, turning away. Jessica sagged, the fight draining out of her, leaving her looking small and broken.

We spent the next few hours in a kind of numb limbo, waiting for showtime. Trying to rehearse "Free to Be" felt pointless, the air still too thick with unspoken things, the emotional subtext now deafeningly loud, at least to some of us. Jessica barely played, just picked at her strings listlessly, staring at her hands. Gemini stared holes in the wall, her jaw tight. Leo kept sighing dramatically, tapping restless rhythms on his trumpet case. Even Rhys seemed to finally sense the mood, retreating into the safe glow of his phone screen. The rejected costumes hung silently on the rack in the corner, a garish reminder of the image they wanted us to project.

Just before we were scheduled to head towards the stage, another official appeared at our door. Not the producer this time, not the wardrobe vultures, but someone sterner, older, wearing a standard grey Sterling Corp suit that screamed 'mid-level bureaucrat with enforcement power.' He carried a tablet and had an air of tired, seen-it-all authority.

"Jessica's Jones," he stated flatly, his eyes scanning the room, taking in our decidedly non-coordinated, non-shiny clothes – our usual ripped jeans, band shirts, boots. "Wardrobe advises you declined the provided performance attire?" His tone was clipped, disapproving, like a drill sergeant inspecting sloppy recruits.

Before anyone else could react, before Leo could launch into another tirade or Jessica could shrink further into herself, I spoke, keeping my voice level, neutral, meeting his gaze directly. "O.B.E."

The official frowned, blinking, the acronym clearly not part of his corporate training manual. "Excuse me? What does that mean?"

"Overcome By Events," I clarified calmly, holding his gaze. Military shorthand. Situation changed, prior directives irrelevant due to unforeseen circumstances – like a sudden outbreak of good taste, or maybe just the fact that the costumes were hideous. Let him figure it out. Or not. Didn't matter. It bought us a few seconds, shifted the dynamic slightly.

He made a small 'tsk' sound under his breath, tapping something dismissively onto his tablet – noting our non-compliance, no doubt, filing it away for future reference. Then his gaze shifted, moving past our clothes, settling on Gemini's bass, specifically on the worn sticker near the bridge. His eyes narrowed slightly. "There's been a flag regarding non-compliant political messaging," he continued, his tone hardening, shifting from bureaucratic annoyance to direct enforcement. "Item 4B: the sticker on the bass guitar. 'This Machine Kills Fascists'." He looked directly at Gemini, pinning her with his gaze. "That needs to be removed prior to taking the stage. It violates Competition Code Section 12, Subsection C: Prohibition of Incendiary or Divisive Imagery." He paused, then added, with a chilling lack of inflection, "Mr. Sterling himself expects a certain standard of decorum and adherence to GLAMA's community values. This competition reflects those values." The implication was clear: this wasn't just some low-level functionary; this directive came from the top. Comply, or face consequences far beyond simple disqualification. Disappearances weren't unheard of.

Gemini stiffened, her hand instinctively going to the sticker, covering it protectively. "It's a historical quote," she said, her voice dangerously level, calm on the surface but vibrating with suppressed fury underneath. "Woody Guthrie."

The official waved a dismissive hand, utterly uninterested in context or history. "Historical context is irrelevant in the current security climate. Standards & Practices deems it potentially inflammatory. It promotes discord." He used the approved buzzwords like weapons, blunt instruments designed to shut down thought. "This competition is about unity, celebrating GLAMA." He paused, letting the implied threat hang in the air. "Remove it, or your band forfeits its place in the Semi-Finals. Immediately." The threat was blunt, unambiguous. No corporate doublespeak this time. Just the raw exercise of power.

I saw the fury flash in Gemini's eyes, the stubborn, defiant set of her jaw. She wasn't going to back down easily. This wasn't just a sticker; it was a symbol, her personal declaration of war. Leo took an angry step forward, opening his mouth, ready to jump into the fray, consequences be damned, but I shot him a sharp warning look across the room. *Not now. Not this battle. Wrong time, wrong place.* Pick your fights. Survive to fight again. Engaging here was tactical suicide.

"Gem," Jessica whispered, her voice shaking, placing a trembling hand on Gemini's arm. "Please. Just… just take it off. It's not worth it. Please, Gem." The fear in her eyes was stark, absolute, amplified by the earlier confession, by the producer's threat, by Sal's arrest, by the lockdown, by the martial law outside. She looked utterly terrified, on the verge of shattering completely. Rhys, for his part, looked almost relieved, nodding subtly in agreement with the official. "Yeah, Gem," he muttered, "it's just a sticker. Don't make a scene." His alignment with the authorities, his dismissal of her core symbol, was another nail in the coffin of band unity.

Gemini looked from the official's implacable, bureaucratic face to Jessica's pleading, frightened one. I saw the internal struggle play out in the tightening of her jaw, the flicker in her eyes – the conflict between defiance and protection. Protecting the band, yes, but mostly, protecting Jessica. With a low curse under her breath, a sound of pure, visceral rage and frustration, her face tight with humiliation, Gemini slowly, deliberately peeled the worn sticker off her bass. It came off in ragged pieces, tearing, leaving behind a faint, sticky outline, like a scar. She crumpled the pieces tightly in her fist, her knuckles white, refusing to look at the official, refusing to give him the satisfaction of seeing her defeat.

The official nodded once, sharply, satisfied. "Excellent. Cooperation is appreciated." He made another note on his tablet. "Proceed to Stage A when called." He turned crisply and left, leaving a toxic silence in his wake.

Gemini stood there, staring at the empty space on her bass where the sticker had been, her fist still clenched around its destroyed remains. She looked smaller somehow, diminished, the fire banked, replaced by a cold, simmering anger. Jessica reached out tentatively, touching her arm again, murmuring something soft I couldn't hear, but Gemini flinched away, turning her back, unable or unwilling to accept comfort, needing to process the violation alone. Rhys just looked relieved that another potential conflict had been averted, still not grasping the significance of what had just been taken.

Watching it all, a cold, hard knot formed in my gut. I'd seen this before. Not on a stage, maybe, but in basic training, overseas. The petty abuses of power designed to break spirits. The stripping away of individuality, the symbols that gave people strength. The demands for compliance under threat, leveraging fear against loyalty. The way fear could paralyze good people, make them compromise their core beliefs just to survive the next minute, the next hour. Seeing Gemini forced to remove that sticker – *her* symbol, *her* declaration – seeing Jessica's raw terror used as a weapon against her, seeing Leo's contained rage and Rhys's oblivious relief... something shifted inside me. My usual pragmatic detachment, my focus on just doing the job, keeping the beat steady, protecting the unit – it wasn't enough anymore. The unit itself was under attack, being dismantled from the inside out by fear and compromise, and from the outside by Sterling's relentless machine. My neutrality, my carefully maintained professional distance, felt like complicity now. It felt like cowardice.

My job was to keep the rhythm, hold the foundation steady. Protect the unit. But sometimes, maybe the rhythm needed to change. Sometimes, the only way to protect the unit was to break the rules, to disrupt the cadence they expected. An internal switch flipped. A decision, cold and clear and irrevocable, settled in my mind. I didn't know how or when, but if things went sideways on that stage tonight, if the fear finally broke Jessica, if the machine tried to crush us completely... I wouldn't just keep the beat. I'd change it. I'd give them a rhythm they wouldn't forget.

CHAPTER 11: GEMINI

The walk from the holding room to the stage felt like marching towards an execution. Or maybe, I tried to tell myself, like walking away from one. The beige hallways seemed longer tonight, the air colder, the silence heavier, charged with unspoken words and the low hum of the building's security systems. We moved together, but we were fractured, broken pieces barely holding a shape. Jessica walked beside me, her face pale and set, eyes staring straight ahead, avoiding mine. Her knuckles were white where she gripped her guitar case. Leo walked slightly behind us, trumpet held tight, his usual bounce replaced by a coiled tension, like a spring wound too tight. Rhys trailed even further back, deliberately separate, his expression a mixture of sullen resentment and nervous energy. And Mack brought up the rear, her footsteps steady, measured, her face unreadable, but I sensed the coiled readiness in her posture, the same watchful intensity she'd had facing down the Iron Eagle frontman.

My own hands felt clammy. My bass felt too light, unbalanced, wrong. The spot where the sticker used to be felt like a raw wound, a phantom limb aching with its absence. *This Machine Kills Fascists.* They hadn't just removed a sticker; they'd tried to remove the intent, the meaning, the *why*. They wanted us declawed, defanged, domesticated. Playing "Free to Be" now, after everything – the Harmony Act, Sal's arrest, the producer's threats, the sticker removal – felt like the ultimate act of surrender. A betrayal of the music, of Leo's vulnerability, of Jessica's fear, even of my own reluctant decision to fight back in the first place. It tasted like defeat.

But maybe, just maybe, it was also the escape hatch. The *cage door* was closing – the lyric approvals, the wardrobe demands, the threats, Sal. We'd agreed we'd bolt when that happened. Maybe *this* was bolting? Playing the safe song, the one they expected, the one that let us walk out of here tonight without escalating things further, without getting disappeared like Sal almost did? Maybe this wasn't giving up the whole fight, just... getting out of this specific, rigged battle? Get out of *this* cage, get back to the real stages, the dive bars, the warehouses, where maybe our words could actually land without being pre-approved by Sterling's thought police. It was a bitter rationalization, I knew that. A way to swallow the compromise. Protecting Jessica was paramount, yes – seeing her terror after I stupidly blurted out my feelings solidified that. But maybe protecting her also meant getting us *out* of this toxic spotlight, and playing "Free to Be" was the fastest, quietest way to the exit. It still felt like shit. It still felt like losing. But maybe it was losing smart, to survive. For now.

As we reached the wings, the roar of the crowd hit us, a wave of sound that wasn't cheering, exactly, but a low, expectant rumble. It sounded... hungry. Menacing. The stage lights spilled out, blindingly bright after the dim hallway. Stagehands in Sterling™ crew shirts scurried around, checking cables, positioning cameras. The air smelled of ozone, dry ice, and expensive hairspray.

"Five minutes, Jessica's Jones!" a stage manager barked into a headset, barely glancing at us.

We took our places on the stage, the familiar positions feeling alien under the intense scrutiny. The vast darkness of the auditorium stretched out before us, punctuated by the glowing red eyes of the SNN cameras. I could feel the weight of unseen eyes watching, judging. The Sterling executives in the front row looked bored, impatient.

Jessica plugged in her guitar, her hands trembling slightly. Leo lifted his trumpet, taking a deep, shaky breath. Rhys avoided looking at any of us, staring intently at his pedalboard. Mack settled behind her kit, a silent, steady presence in the storm.

I plugged in my bass, the raw spot where the sticker used to be burning under my fingers. I looked over at Jessica. Her eyes were squeezed shut, her face tight with fear. She looked breakable. My decision back in the room solidified, twisted into this new shape: Play it safe. Get her out of here. Get *us* out of here. We could figure out the rest later. If there was a later.

Mack clicked her sticks together. One. Two. Three. Four.

We launched into "Free to Be." The opening chords felt hesitant, shaky. My bassline felt sluggish, unwilling. Leo's opening trumpet fanfare lacked its usual bright confidence. Rhys's rhythm guitar was technically correct but lacked any drive.

Then I started singing. "Walkin' round in little squares... Breathing' someone else's airs..." My voice felt thin, strained. The words, once a coded declaration of hope and yearning, now tasted like ashes in my mouth. Singing them here, now, felt like a lie, a performance of compliance.

We got to the first chorus. "Don't you wanna be free to be? Just free to be, authentically?" The irony was a physical pain in my chest.

Then it happened. Jessica's part. The intricate guitar line that usually soared, weaving around my vocals. Tonight, her fingers fumbled. A wrong note, then another. The rhythm faltered, stumbled. Her eyes flew open, wide with panic. She looked lost, utterly terrified, exposed under the harsh lights. The song, already fragile, started to collapse inwards. The carefully constructed compromise shattered.

In that split second of unraveling, I saw Mack's head snap up. Her gaze, sharp and unwavering, flicked from my own startled expression to Jessica's faltering form, then locked onto Jessica's eyes directly. Mack gave a single, decisive nod to Jessica – a look that cut through the rising panic, a clear, unspoken command to shift gears. Before the song could completely die, before the judges could start scribbling notes about unprofessionalism, before Anderson could smirk in satisfaction, Mack *changed the beat*. Abruptly. Decisively. No warning, just BAM. The steady, mid-tempo ska rhythm vanished, replaced by a driving, pounding, aggressive beat – the heavy, furious heartbeat of "Patriot Games."

The shift was instantaneous, shocking. Rhys's head jerked up, his eyes wide with disbelief, confusion warring with anger. But Leo... Leo didn't hesitate. He recognized the rhythm instantly, the song we'd worked on in secret, the Molotov cocktail we'd agreed was too dangerous. A fierce grin split his face, chasing away the fear. He lifted his trumpet and blasted out the song's jarring, defiant opening riff, loud and clear and utterly unapologetic.

My own fingers found the new bassline automatically, the heavy, distorted groove pouring out of me, fueled by weeks of suppressed rage. But my eyes were locked on Jessica. This was her moment. Her choice. Stay broken, stay safe? Or fight back?

She stood frozen for a heartbeat, caught between the terror that had made her falter and the raw, undeniable power of the music erupting around her. I saw the conflict warring in her eyes. Then, she looked at me. Really looked at me. And something shifted. The fear didn't vanish, but something stronger rose to meet it. Resolve. Anger. Maybe even love. She took a visible breath, nodded almost imperceptibly, and launched into the furious, razor-sharp guitar riff of "Patriot Games," hitting it harder, louder, dirtier than she ever had in practice. She was in. All in.

A surge of adrenaline, fierce and joyful, shot through me. With Jessica committed, with Leo wailing like a revolutionary herald, with Mack laying down a beat like artillery fire, I stepped up to the mic, unleashed. The words poured out, no longer just lyrics on a page, but pure, unadulterated fury given voice.

"Same old story, different screen! Selling nightmares, calling dreams! Got your flag wrapped tight and clean! Hide the dirt that lies between!"

The sound hit the room like a physical force. I saw the Sterling execs in the front row jolt upright, their bored expressions replaced by shock, then anger. The judges stopped scribbling, staring up at us, mouths slightly open. The SNN cameras zoomed in, their red lights burning.

"Billionaire kings on gilded thrones! Chewing futures, sucking bones! Got your mouthpiece? Yeah, it drones! While you tap your shiny phones!"

We tore through the song, a furious wave of noise and rage. Jessica's guitar screamed, Leo's trumpet wailed like an air-raid siren, Mack's drumming was relentless, a controlled explosion. We were feeding off each other, off the danger, off the sheer, liberating audacity of what we were doing.

Then, out of the corner of my eye, I saw Rhys. He stood there, frozen, guitar silent against his chest, his face a mask of shock, betrayal, and maybe disgust. He looked from me to Jessica, then back again, as if finally understanding the subtext he'd missed, filtered through the lens of the Harmony Act, the propaganda, his own insecurities. This wasn't just politics to him anymore; it was personal, twisted into something ugly. He saw our defiance not as resistance, but as recklessness, madness. With a look of finality, he unplugged his guitar cable, letting it drop to the stage with a clatter. He turned his back on us and walked off, disappearing into the wings mid-song. Gone.

We didn't falter. If anything, his departure fueled the fire. We slammed into the bridge, heavier now, angrier.

"No more whispers! No more codes! Time to lighten up these loads! Call it out! Name the game! They feed the fire! Fan the flame! Freedom's Ring? A golden chain! Wash the blood out with the rain? NO!"

As the words ripped from my throat, I saw it happen. One by one, the little red recording lights on the sleek, robotic SNN cameras dotting the stage and the auditorium flickered out. First the one sweeping near the drum riser, then the main one center stage, then another, and another. A silent, coordinated shutdown. The official narrative was being severed. But in the same breath, a different kind of light began to bloom in the darkness of the crowd. Tiny screens, dozens of them, then scores, then what felt like hundreds, held aloft. Phones. Tablets. The audience, the ones not in Sterling's pocket, the ones who hadn't fled, were raising their own cameras, their own lenses. They were recording. Not the sanitized, approved feed, but this. Raw. Unfiltered. It was a small thing, maybe. A fleeting gesture in the face of the state's power. But seeing those individual lights pierce the gloom, a constellation of defiant eyes, it felt like... something. A breath. A possibility. Even if most of the world would see this as just a band imploding, a bunch of kids throwing a tantrum, maybe these small lights meant someone, somewhere, would see more.

Leo took the solo then, not the flashy ska runs, but raw, aggressive blasts of sound, pushing his trumpet to its limits, pouring all his fear and anger and hope into the horn. It was breathtaking.

We crashed into the final chorus, giving it everything we had left.

"THIS! Is your Patriot Games! Your Freedom's Cage! Turn the page! Unleash the RAGE!"

The final chord hit, a wall of distorted sound, followed by an abrupt, shocking silence as Mack cut it dead with a final cymbal crash. We stood there, panting, chests heaving, sweat dripping, defiant under the hot lights.

For a moment, stunned silence hung over the auditorium. Then, chaos erupted. Shouting from the audience – confusion, anger, but also, distinctly, some cheers, some fists raised in solidarity from the back. The judges looked furious, conferring frantically. The Sterling execs were already on their phones, barking orders.

Security guards started moving towards the stage, their faces grim.

But before they could reach us, before the feed inevitably cut, I reached into my back pocket, pulled out the crumpled, torn pieces of the sticker, smoothed them out as best I could, and slapped them defiantly back onto the raw spot on my bass. *This Machine Kills Fascists.* Maybe it did. Maybe it could.

The house lights came up abruptly, harsh and revealing. The stage manager was screaming into his headset. More security flooded the aisles. Time to go. Time to bolt. The cage door wasn't just closing; we'd just kicked it off its hinges. Now we had to run like hell.

CHAPTER 12: GEMINI

The final chord of "Patriot Games" was still ringing in my ears, a phantom vibration against the sudden, harsh glare of the house lights, when the chaos truly erupted. Shouts from the audience – a confusing, angry roar mixed with pockets of defiant cheers that felt miles away, like sounds from another world. The stage manager, his face a mask of contorted panic, was screaming into his headset, spittle flying. Sterling Security guards, their faces grim and set like concrete, were already moving with chilling speed towards the stage from both wings, their movements quick, purposeful, like wolves closing in on wounded prey. The Sterling execs in the front row were on their feet, jabbing fingers, their faces flushed with outrage. The judges, moments before impassive arbiters of taste, now looked like they'd swallowed a collective batch of very sour lemons, conferring frantically.

"Go! Now!" Mack's voice cut through the din, sharp as a razor, urgent. She was already in motion, a blur of efficiency, grabbing her snare and cymbal bag with the practiced economy of someone who had evacuated under fire before. There was no hesitation in her, only focused action.

There was no time to think, only to react. Adrenaline surged, a sickening cocktail of cold dread and hot panic. Leo, his face pale but his eyes blazing, was already by Jessica's side, grabbing her arm. "Jess, come on!" he urged, pulling her towards the backstage exit we'd used to enter, the one leading to the labyrinthine corridors. My own feet felt rooted to the spot for a horrifying second, the image of those approaching guards – their polished boots, the glint of metal on their belts – burning into my brain.

The newly reapplied sticker on my bass felt like a giant, blinking target painted on my back. *This Machine Kills Fascists.* Right now, it felt like this machine was about to get us all killed.

"Gemini! Move!" Mack barked again, her voice a physical force that broke my paralysis. She gave me a hard shove forward, propelling me after Jessica and Leo.

We plunged into the backstage maze, the sounds of pursuit echoing immediately behind us – heavy, rhythmic footsteps pounding on the industrial carpet, shouted commands bouncing off the beige, featureless walls. The corridors, once just oppressively bland, now felt like a closing trap, every identical turn a potential dead end. The air was stale, thick with the smell of fear and old dust.

"Loading dock!" Mack yelled from behind me, somehow having assessed our escape route options in seconds. She pushed past, taking the lead, her movements compact and economical, her head constantly swiveling, eyes scanning every intersection, every shadowed doorway, assessing threats with a speed and precision that spoke of training I didn't want to contemplate. She was in her element, a soldier navigating hostile territory, while the rest of us were just terrified kids.

We burst through a set of heavy double doors, the kind designed to muffle sound, and into the brightly lit, surprisingly clean underground loading bay. It felt like emerging into an operating theater. Jessica's parents' minivan stood there, maybe fifty yards away, a gleaming white beacon of potential escape in the sterile, concrete expanse. But our hope choked in our throats. Between us and the van stood two Sterling Security guards, their stances alert, already turning towards us at the sound of the doors banging open. They'd clearly been alerted by the commotion upstairs. Their hands were already reaching for the sidearms holstered on their belts, their expressions hardening as they registered who we were.

"Shit!" Leo breathed, skidding to a halt on the polished concrete. Jessica whimpered beside him, her eyes wide with a terror so profound it seemed to swallow all other emotion. She looked like a cornered animal.

The guards were shouting, their voices amplified by the acoustics of the bay, "Stop! Right there! Don't move! Hands where we can see them!"

There was no way around them. We were caught. My stomach plummeted, a lead weight dropping through me. This was it. The cage door wasn't just closing; it was slamming shut, locking us in for good. My mind flashed to Sal, to the stories of people disappearing into CPB detention centers. I remembered my deal with Jessica – *bolt if it feels like a cage*. This felt less like a cage and more like a goddamn execution chamber.

But Mack didn't stop. She didn't even hesitate. "Gem, Jess, Leo – get to the van! Start it!" she commanded, her voice calm, cold, utterly authoritative, cutting through my rising panic. Before we could argue, before the guards could fully draw their weapons and take aim, she moved. It wasn't flashy, not like in the movies. It was brutal, efficient, and terrifyingly fast. She closed the distance to the nearest guard in two quick, silent strides, her body low, coiled like a spring. I saw her use the guard's own forward momentum against him as he lunged. A blur of motion – a hand striking upwards to deflect his draw, a sharp, sickening crack as her elbow connected with his jaw. A grunt of pain as he stumbled back, eyes rolling, disoriented. She didn't wait to see him fall. She was already pivoting, a whirlwind of controlled force, dealing with the second guard who was now fumbling to unholster his weapon, his eyes wide with a mixture of surprise and dawning fear. Mack used a heavy-duty metal mic stand she must have grabbed from backstage – when had she even done that? – as a makeshift quarterstaff. A swift, disabling strike to his weapon arm, a yelp of pain, and then a hard, leveraged shove that sent him sprawling into a stack of empty, clattering equipment cases. It was over in seconds. Two armed guards, neutralized, groaning on the floor.

"Go!" she repeated, her voice tight, already scanning the entrance to the loading bay, anticipating more threats.

We scrambled towards the minivan, adrenaline making my fingers clumsy and unresponsive on the door handle. Jessica fumbled with the keys, her hands shaking so violently she could barely fit the key fob into the ignition slot. Leo was beside her, trying to calm her, his own voice strained. "Easy, Jess, easy. You got this. Just breathe." I threw my bass into the back, the defiant white of the sticker a stark contrast against the black finish of the instrument. It felt less like a statement now and more like evidence.

The engine finally roared to life with a cough and a sputter, just as more shouts echoed from the corridor we'd just exited. Mack dived into the passenger seat, slamming the door shut with a resonant thud. "Drive, Jess! Drive! Ramp! Now!"

Jessica stomped on the accelerator. The minivan, designed for sedate suburban errands, lurched forward with an uncharacteristic squeal of tires on the smooth concrete floor of the loading bay. It careened, fishtailing slightly, towards the wide exit ramp that led up to the street level and, hopefully, some semblance of escape. My phone, forgotten in my pocket during the on-stage chaos and the desperate flight, started buzzing frantically, a frantic, insistent vibration against my leg, like an angry trapped insect.

As we shot up the ramp, the tires momentarily losing traction, and burst out into the chaotic glare of the city night, the change in atmosphere was jarring. Sirens wailed, a discordant symphony from every direction. The air was thick with tension, acrid with the smell of something burning – tires? chemicals? – and the distant, unsettling pop-pop-pop of what might have been tear gas launchers or worse. Red and blue emergency lights strobed across the cityscape, painting familiar buildings in lurid, unfamiliar colors. GLAMA looked like a city under siege.

I fumbled for the phone, my heart leaping into my throat as I saw the caller ID. Mom.

"Gemini? Oh, thank God! Gemini, are you there?" Her voice was a choked sob, laced with a terror I'd never heard from her in my life. Static crackled on the line, making her words distort.

"Mom? Mom, what's wrong? Are you okay?" My own voice sounded thin, reedy.

"They're here, baby! At the house! The CPB... they're... they're *detaining* your father!" A muffled shout in the background – Dad's voice, loud, angry, confused. "They say it's for *immigration violations!*" Mom's voice cracked with disbelief and fury. "But that's impossible, Gem, your father was born right here in GLAMA! His parents were born here! It's a lie! A pretext!" Then her voice broke, dissolving into tears. "They're asking about you, Gem! About the band! About what you did tonight! They said... they said you're inciting rebellion!"

Inciting rebellion. Immigration violations. The words twisted in my gut. It was so blatant, so transparently false. Using the CPB, the arm of the state designed to terrorize immigrants, against a citizen whose family had been here for generations. It was a chilling message: no one was safe. Any law could be twisted, any agency weaponized, to silence dissent, to punish those who stepped out of line. My father, whose only crime was being *my* father. The guilt was a cold, heavy stone in my stomach. This wasn't just about a sticker anymore, or a song, or getting kicked out of a competition. This was the state coming down, hard. They were coming for my family. Because of me.

"Gemini, listen to me!" Mom's voice was suddenly sharp, desperate, cutting through my shock. "You can't come home! Do you understand? You can't! They're waiting for you! You have to run, baby! Run far away! Don't let them catch you! Please, Gemini, promise me you'll run!" The line crackled again, a burst of harsh static, and then went dead.

"Mom? Mom!" I screamed into the phone, but there was only silence. I stared at the blank screen, confused, my thumb jabbing uselessly at the call button. Then, a message flashed across the dark glass, stark white letters against a black background: CONNECTION TERMINATED. DEVICE LOCKED BY STERLING SECURENET.

"What's wrong?" Mack's voice cut through my daze. She'd twisted in the passenger seat, her eyes sharp, missing nothing.

"The call... it just crashed," I stammered, still staring at the chilling message. "It says... locked?"

Before I could process it further, Mack's hand shot out, snatching the phone from my grasp with surprising speed. "Everyone. Phones. Now." Her voice was flat, devoid of emotion, but carried an undeniable authority.

"What? Why?" Leo asked, startled, but he was already reaching into his pocket. Jessica, her face a pale mask of fear, fumbled in her bag.

Mack didn't explain, just held out her hand, palm up. One by one, we handed them over. She took mine, Leo's, then Jessica's. Without a word, she rolled down her window, the sudden rush of night air and distant sirens filling the van. And then, with a swift, decisive motion, she threw all three phones out into the darkness. They disappeared, swallowed by the night.

"Mack! What the hell?" Leo exclaimed, twisting around to stare after them. "My contacts! My photos!"

"OpSec," Mack stated, rolling the window back up. Her eyes met mine in the rearview mirror, hard and unyielding. "Those phones are a liability. Trackers. Listening devices. Sterling SecureNet? That means they own the network, they own the devices. They were probably listening to your mom's call, Gem. They know we're in this van. They know where we might be going." She paused, letting the weight of her words sink in. "From now on, we go dark. No digital footprint. They're an operational security threat to this... this group. And right now, the survival of this group is the only mission that matters."

The minivan swerved violently as Jessica, her hands gripping the wheel so tight her knuckles were white, navigated through streets that felt like a warzone. She ran a red light, narrowly avoiding a collision with a CPB armored personnel carrier that was rumbling through the intersection, its black paintjob absorbing the light, its presence utterly menacing.

"Jess! Watch it!" Leo yelled, gripping the dashboard.

"Should I floor it? Try to lose them if they saw us?" Jessica cried, her voice cracking, eyes darting frantically between the road and the rearview mirror.

"No!" Mack's voice was sharp, cutting through Jessica's panic. "Drive normally. As normally as you can in this mess. Don't draw attention. They're looking for chaos, don't give it to them. One wrong move and we're boxed in." She was scanning behind us, her head moving methodically. "Think they made us?"

"I don't know! I don't know!" Jessica sobbed. "That APC... it was right there!"

"It kept going," Mack said, her voice a sliver calmer. "But there are patrols everywhere. We need to get off these main streets."

I stared out the window, the city lights blurring past, the weight of Mack's actions, of Mom's terrified words, pressing down on me. *Locked by Sterling SecureNet.* They owned everything. My dad... detained on a bullshit charge. Because of me. The guilt was a cold, heavy stone in my stomach. But Mom's words were a burning brand: *Run.*

"Turn here," Mack ordered, pointing down a narrow, unlit side street. "Get us into the industrial district. More places to disappear if we need to."

Jessica wrenched the wheel, the van bumping over a curb. We plunged into darker streets, the wail of sirens momentarily receding. The industrial district was a maze of looming warehouses, their windows dark and vacant like empty eye sockets, and shuttered factories that smelled of old chemicals and decay. Jessica, her face a pale mask in the dashboard's glow, drove with a jerky, uncertain rhythm, her knuckles white on the steering wheel. Her breath came in shallow gasps. She was running on pure adrenaline and terror, and I worried she was just going through familiar motions, her mind too fractured to truly process Mack's directions.

"Jess, you okay? This the right way?" Leo asked gently from the passenger seat, his voice laced with concern.

Jessica didn't answer, just made another sharp turn, then another, her driving becoming more erratic. The streets here were poorly lit, pocked with potholes that jarred the minivan violently. It felt like we were driving in circles, lost in a concrete wasteland.

"Mack, where are we?" I asked, leaning forward, trying to peer through the grimy windshield. The landscape of rust-colored brick and corrugated metal felt disorienting, alien.

Before Mack could answer, Leo let out a choked sound. "Oh, no. Jess... stop."

We rounded a familiar corner, the one with the perpetually overflowing dumpster and the faded mural of a mythical sea creature, and there it was. The Rat Hole. Or what was left of it. The flickering neon sign depicting the guitar-playing rat was dark, smashed. The front windows were boarded up with raw, splintered plywood. Yellow CPB tape, stark and official under the sickly orange glow of a lone streetlight, crisscrossed the entrance like a grotesque X. A large, official-looking notice, printed on cheap paper and already peeling at the edges, was stapled to the boarded-up door. Even from the van, I could make out the bold, impersonal lettering: PREMISES SEIZED BY ORDER OF

THE CITIZEN PROTECTION BUREAU. UNAUTHORIZED ENTRY PROHIBITED. VIOLATORS WILL BE PROSECUTED.

Jessica slammed on the brakes, the minivan skidding to a halt in the middle of the deserted street. She stared at the club, her face ashen, tears silently tracing paths through the grime on her cheeks. "Sal..." she whispered, her voice cracking. This was where we'd played our first real gigs, where we'd found our sound, our community. It was supposed to be a haven, a grimy, defiant sanctuary. Now it was just another casualty, another piece of our lives boarded up and branded by the state.

"They didn't just warn him," Leo said, his voice hollow, devoid of its usual energy. "They shut him down. For us." The weight of that, the direct consequence of our actions on someone who had tried to help us, settled heavily in the van, another layer of guilt and despair.

"Another bridge burned," Mack stated grimly, her eyes scanning the darkened alleyways around the club, assessing for threats. "No going back there. Not for any of us."

I looked at the boarded-up club, the official notice a stark symbol of the regime's reach. Sal, who just wanted to run his dive bar and give bands a place to play, was now a target, his livelihood destroyed, probably facing charges himself. My dad was in a CPB holding cell. Our phones were gone. We were fugitives in our own city. The realization hit with the force of a physical blow: every connection, every safe space we thought we had in GLAMA, was either compromised or gone. There was truly nowhere left to turn.

Jessica let out a shuddering sob, her shoulders shaking. "It's my fault," she choked out. "If I hadn't pushed for the competition... if we hadn't..."

"No," I said, my voice surprisingly firm, cutting through her self-blame. "It's not your fault, Jess. It's theirs. All of it." I looked from the shuttered club to the faces of my bandmates, illuminated by the faint dashboard lights – Jessica's despair, Leo's grim

127

resignation, Mack's watchful intensity. The anger, cold and sharp, cut through my own fear. "They want us to blame ourselves. To go quiet in our shame. They want us to fall apart. We can't let them."

Mack nodded slowly. "Gemini's right. Recriminations are a luxury we don't have. We need to keep moving. This area isn't secure." She pointed down another dark street. "That way. Towards the freeway interchanges. We need to get out of the city core before they lock it down completely."

Jessica took a deep, shuddering breath, wiping her eyes with the back of her hand. She put the van in drive, her movements still shaky but more purposeful now. The image of The Rat Hole, boarded up and violated, seemed to solidify something in her, a grim resolve replacing the raw panic. We pulled away from the curb, leaving Sal's silenced club behind us, another ghost in a city rapidly filling with them.

The van was quiet for a long stretch, the only sounds the hum of the engine and the occasional sniffle from Jessica. The adrenaline was wearing off, leaving behind a bone-deep exhaustion and a gnawing dread. We were truly on our own. Fugitives. The word felt heavy, unreal.

"So," Leo said finally, his voice flat, breaking the silence. "Rhys. He just... walked." It wasn't a question, more a statement of bewildered fact.

The image of Rhys turning his back, unplugging his guitar, flashed in my mind. The anger I'd felt on stage had cooled, leaving behind something more complicated. "Yeah," I said, my voice tired. "He did."

"Can't say I blame him," Jessica mumbled, her voice thick with unshed tears. "We were reckless. We put everyone in danger."

"He made his choice, Jess," I said, trying to keep the bitterness out of my voice. "He chose... not us. Not this." I thought of his disgusted look when I'd blurted out my feelings for Jessica, the way he'd sided with the official about the sticker. It wasn't just fear that made him walk; it was judgment. He didn't get it. He didn't want to get it. "His fear, his... issues... that's on him. He was always looking for an easy way, for approval from the wrong people. He found it, I guess." A part of me, the part that remembered him awkwardly trying to fit in, the part that saw his genuine musical talent, felt a pang of something like sadness. But it was quickly overshadowed by the sharper sting of betrayal. He'd absorbed the propaganda, the hate, and when the pressure hit, he'd folded, turned on us.

"He was scared," Leo said quietly. "We all are. But he didn't have to be an asshole about it."

"He was always susceptible," Mack added, her voice neutral from the front seat. "Listened to the wrong narratives. Saw the competition as a ladder, not a cage. When it got too real, he bailed."

The conversation about Rhys died there, another casualty of the night. He was gone. Another piece of our old lives severed. We drove on in silence for a while, the city lights receding behind us. The weight of what we'd done, what had been done to us, settled in. My dad. Sal. The band, fractured. Our lives, upended.

The air in the van grew thick with unspoken fear and exhaustion. Jessica, beside me, was trembling almost constantly now, her earlier resolve crumbling. I could feel the tremors through the seat. She stared straight ahead, her eyes wide and unfocused, lost in a terror I could only imagine. The weight of my earlier confession, the one that had ripped out of me in the holding room, felt like a physical barrier between us now, an added complication to the already impossible situation. I wanted to reach out, to say something, anything, but the words wouldn't come. What could I say? *Sorry I might have just made our lives even more dangerous?*

It was Mack who finally broke the silence, her voice cutting through the heavy atmosphere, pulling us back to the immediate, brutal reality. "We need a plan," she said, her tone flat, practical, from the front seat. "Not just for tonight, but for the next few days. Leo, those Canadian contacts. How solid are they?"

Leo sighed, the sound heavy with weariness. He ran a hand through his already disheveled hair. "Solid enough, I hope. But getting there... that's the problem. We're on our own. No phones, no money to speak of, and probably half of GLAMA PD and the entire CPB looking for us by now."

"We need to get out of GLAMA," I said, the words tasting like ash in my mouth. "Tonight. We can't stay here." My mom's terrified voice, her desperate plea, echoed in my head. *Run, baby!*

"Agreed," Mack said. "North. Canada is the only viable option. It's a long shot, but it's the only shot we have."

The decision hung in the air, heavy and irrevocable. Flee. Become fugitives. Leave everything behind. It was insane. It was terrifying. It was the only thing left to do.

CHAPTER 13: GEMINI

The industrial district dissolved behind us into a rearview mirror smeared with grime and the reflected glare of distant, chaotic lights. The smell of burning chemicals and old decay faded, replaced by the generic, slightly stale air recirculating inside the minivan. Jessica was still at the wheel, her knuckles white, eyes darting between the road and the mirrors with a frantic energy that seemed unsustainable. Mack rode shotgun, a grim navigator scanning the darkness, her posture radiating a coiled readiness that was both reassuring and terrifying.

Leo and I were crammed in the middle row, the leather seat sticking uncomfortably to my skin. The space behind us, usually packed tight with amps and Mack's meticulously organized drum kit, now felt cavernously empty, holding only our naked instruments – my bass, Jessica's guitar, Leo's trumpet, all hastily thrown in without cases – and the heavy-duty mic stand Mack had somehow acquired and wielded as a weapon during our escape. It lay there, cold and metallic, a stark testament to what we'd fled and what we'd been forced to leave behind. Our sound, our gear, our history – all abandoned on the stage of Sterling's monument to himself. Jessica, guided by Mack's terse directions, navigated the minivan through a bewildering maze of service roads and darkened underpasses, finally merging onto the northbound I-5. The freeway was eerily empty for this time of night, the usual relentless river of headlights thinned to a trickle. Martial law had choked the city's arteries. Every overpass loomed like a potential checkpoint, a concrete shadow under which unseen eyes might be watching.

Then we saw it.

On the southbound side of the freeway, heading *into* GLAMA, a sight so surreal and terrifying it felt torn from a dystopian nightmare. A massive convoy. Dozens, maybe hundreds, of military-style vehicles – not just the black CPB armored personnel carriers we'd glimpsed earlier, but heavy-duty troop transports, Humvee-equivalents painted in drab olive, and several flat-bed carriers loaded with what looked like actual light tanks or urban assault vehicles, their silhouettes stark and menacing against the hazy orange glow of the city lights.

Their headlights cut through the darkness in a relentless, unified column, stretching back as far as the eye could see, an endless river of steel and implied force flowing into the heart of the city we were so desperately trying to flee. National Guard? CPB's elite tactical units? Some newly deputized Sterling private army? It didn't matter. It was the physical manifestation of martial law, of Sterling's fist closing around GLAMA. It was the boot, preparing to stomp.

A profound, visceral chill snaked down my spine, colder than the failing air conditioning. My breath caught in my throat. *Fuck, am I glad we're going this way.* The thought was sharp, involuntary, a raw instinct for self-preservation. We were minnows swimming against a tidal wave, escaping just as the full, crushing weight of the state bore down. The object thrown at Sterling's press conference, the supposed "security incident" – it felt like a flimsy pretext now, a convenient excuse manufactured or seized upon with chilling speed. This level of mobilization, this overwhelming show of force... it couldn't have been scrambled in a few hours. This felt planned. Orchestrated. Sterling hadn't just reacted; he'd been waiting for an opportunity, a trigger, and someone had handed it to him. He was squeezing the city, purging the dissent, consolidating control under the guise of restoring order, and we were barely slipping through his closing fingers.

Silence, thick and heavy, filled the van as the last of the convoy's taillights disappeared behind us, a receding tide of menace. The image burned itself into my mind – the endless line of olive drab, the faceless drivers, the sheer weight of state power rolling inexorably towards the lives we'd just abandoned. The silence was broken only by the hum of the tires on the asphalt and Jessica's ragged, uneven breathing. The adrenaline from the escape, from Mack's brutal efficiency in the loading dock, from my mother's terrified call, had leached away, leaving behind a bone-deep weariness and a gnawing, hollow fear. My father. Detained. Because of me. The words replayed in my head, a soundtrack to the desolate landscape scrolling past the windows. Sal's boarded-up club. The Sterling SecureNet message on my dead phone. Mack tossing our digital lifelines out the window. Every bridge to our old lives felt like it was not just burned, but nuked from orbit. We were adrift, cut off, ghosts fleeing a city that was actively trying to erase us.

We drove north, into the deepening night, away from the smoldering chaos of GLAMA. After another hour of tense, near-silent driving, Jessica's shoulders began to slump, her head nodding almost imperceptibly. "Pull over at the next wide spot," Mack said quietly from the passenger seat. "You're done, Jess. I'll take it from here." Jessica didn't argue, just numbly guided the van to the gravel shoulder. The exchange was quick, efficient. Mack slid into the driver's seat, her movements economical even in the cramped space. Leo, who had been quiet in the middle row with me, moved up to take the passenger seat, his face pale in the dashboard lights but his eyes alert, ready to help navigate or watch for trouble. Jessica stumbled into the middle row, collapsing onto the bench seat beside me, her body trembling with exhaustion.

Hours passed in a blur of identical freeway signs, anonymous truck stops flickering past in the darkness like lonely, neon-lit islands in an ocean of night, and the monotonous drone of the engine under Mack's steady hand. Paranoia was a constant companion, coiling in my stomach with every distant siren, every pair of headlights that lingered too long in the rearview mirror before finally veering off onto an exit ramp. Was that flickering light a patrol car turning around? Was the driver of that semi watching us too closely? Every shadow seemed to hold a threat. Were they looking for us? Were our faces already plastered across some internal CPB bulletin? Was Sterling himself, in his gilded tower, orchestrating the hunt? The not knowing was a particular kind of torture, feeding the fear, making the silence in the van feel heavier, more charged.

Mack, now driving, used an old-fashioned paper map she'd produced from somewhere in her duffel bag, its creases worn, its edges soft from use. She navigated with quiet competence, her eyes flicking between the road, the map illuminated by a small penlight held by Leo, and the rearview mirror. She directed us onto smaller state highways, avoiding the main interstate where checkpoints were more likely. The roads grew darker, narrower, winding through agricultural valleys that smelled of damp earth and fertilizer, a thick, organic scent that felt both alien and strangely grounding after the metallic tang of fear and smog in GLAMA. Then we climbed into hills shrouded in mist, the air growing cooler, the trees closing in, their branches dripping with moisture, making the world outside the minivan feel close and secretive. The landscape felt ancient, indifferent to our frantic flight, a silent witness to countless other journeys, other escapes.

Sometime before dawn, as a pale, bruised light began to seep into the eastern sky, staining the mist a sickly grey, Mack, still at the wheel, her face etched with fatigue but her eyes still sharp, directed us to pull off onto a deserted dirt track leading into a dense grove of eucalyptus trees. The track was barely visible, overgrown with weeds. "We rest here," she announced, her voice low, but firm. "Everyone's exhausted. Can't make mistakes. Need clear heads for the next leg."

The silence when Mack cut the engine was profound, almost deafening after the hours of engine drone. Broken only by the chirping of unseen crickets and the rustle of leaves in the faint breeze. It felt like we were the only people left on earth, hidden away in this pocket of damp, fragrant wilderness. The air was cool, carrying the sharp, medicinal scent of eucalyptus and wet soil, a world away from the choking atmosphere of GLAMA.

We didn't talk much. There were no words adequate for the enormity of what had happened, what we'd lost, the chasm that had opened between our lives yesterday and our reality now. Leo managed to produce a crushed bag of trail mix – mostly dust and a few lonely-looking peanuts – and a couple of lukewarm bottles of water from his backpack. We shared them in silence, huddled in the cramped minivan, the small act of communion feeling almost sacred in its normalcy. Jessica, now slumped beside me in the middle row, her head resting limply against the window, took a bottle with trembling hands. She fumbled with the cap, her fingers clumsy with exhaustion and shock. I reached over, my fingers brushing hers – a spark of static electricity, or maybe something else – and took it, unscrewing the cap for her. She gave me a small, grateful look, her eyes shadowed with exhaustion and a pain that mirrored my own. The unspoken words from the holding room, my accidental confession, hung between us, unaddressed, too raw, too dangerous to touch, yet somehow less important than this shared moment of weary survival.

I tried to sleep, curled uncomfortably against the van door, Jessica a warm, fragile weight against me. Her proximity was both a comfort and an agony, a reminder of the connection that felt both more real and more impossible than ever. My mind wouldn't shut down. Images replayed behind my eyelids: the SNN cameras going dark, the sea of phone lights in the crowd like defiant stars, Mack moving with lethal grace in the loading dock, my mother's terrified face on the phone screen, the CPB tape across Sal's door like a wound. My father. The guilt was a physical ache, a cold knot tightening in my stomach. I pulled out my sketchbook, the one thing I'd managed to grab besides my bass. The pen felt awkward in my tired hand, the cheap paper rough under my fingers, but I needed to process, to make some mark, any mark, against the overwhelming darkness.

The lines that emerged on the page were jagged, uncertain. Not faces, not caricatures, but abstract shapes, broken lines, the feeling of static, of displacement, of being untethered. *Engine hums a low-down tune... Underneath a busted moon... White lines flicker, hypnotize... Reflecting tired in your eyes...* The words started to form in my head, a counter-melody to the fear, weaving through the exhaustion. A bassline, slow and mournful, a heartbeat in the dark, began to pulse in my inner ear, a rhythm for the road, for the flight north. *Static crackles on the air... Whispering words of who knows where... Miles dissolving in the black... No map showing the way back...*

Mack took the first watch, sitting bolt upright in the driver's seat, motionless as stone, her eyes scanning the tree line, alert even in exhaustion. Leo eventually drifted into a restless sleep in the passenger seat, his head lolling against the window, soft snores escaping his lips, a sound incongruously peaceful amidst the wreckage of our lives. Jessica finally succumbed too, her breathing evening out, though small, troubled sounds occasionally escaped her lips, whimpers caught between sleep and nightmare. Her head rested on my shoulder, a fragile weight, her dark hair tickling my cheek. Despite everything, despite the fear and the uncertainty and the crushing guilt, a wave of fierce, protective tenderness washed over me. I carefully shifted, trying not to disturb her, letting her sleep, guarding this small moment of peace.

As the sun climbed higher, painting the sky in shades of bruised purple and reluctant orange, filtering weakly through the dense eucalyptus canopy, Mack woke us with a quiet nudge. "Time to move," she said, her voice raspy with fatigue. "Can't stay in one place too long. Too exposed."

The journey resumed, a monotonous cycle of driving, watching, rationing dwindling snacks, and the oppressive weight of unspoken fears. Mack drove again, her endurance seemingly superhuman, though the lines around her eyes were deeper now. Leo sat beside her, scanning the map, occasionally pointing out a turnoff onto an even more obscure county road. The minivan, coated in a layer of dust that offered a small measure of camouflage, stuck to back roads, avoiding anything that looked like a major artery or a potential checkpoint. Each gas station stop felt like a high-stakes gamble, Leo or Mack going in quickly, hoods up, faces down, paying cash for gas and maybe a few bags of chips, while Jessica and I waited in the van, hearts pounding, scanning every approaching car, every lingering gaze, for any sign of trouble.

The landscape changed again. The rolling hills gave way to flatter, more arid terrain, the sun beating down relentlessly through the windshield. Then we climbed into the stark, majestic desolation of the high desert, a vast expanse of sand, scrub, and distant, heat-hazed mountains under an enormous, unforgiving sky. The van's air conditioning, never robust, finally gave up the ghost, turning the interior into a stuffy, uncomfortable oven.

Tempers frayed in the heat and confinement. Leo and I got into a hushed, bitter argument over whether to risk turning on the radio for news, him desperate for any scrap of information about GLAMA, about potential pursuit, me terrified of anything that could give away our position or shatter the fragile illusion of escape. "We need to know what they're saying, Gem!" he hissed, his voice tight with frustration. "We need intel!" "Intel isn't worth getting caught, Leo!" I whispered back fiercely. "What if they're tracking broadcasts? What if hearing more lies just makes it worse?" We lapsed into sullen silence, the argument unresolved, the tension simmering between us. Jessica remained mostly silent through it all, staring out the window, a ghost of her former self, her eyes haunted, occasionally tracing patterns on the dusty glass with a fingertip.

During one tense stop for gas in a dusty, forgotten town that felt like it hadn't changed since the 1950s – tumbleweeds, a blinking yellow light, a general store with faded paint – I saw a news kiosk outside the gas station mini-mart. My heart leaped, then sank. Against my better judgment, while Mack paid inside, I drifted closer, scanning the headlines. The headline of a GLAMA-based paper, days old but still screaming from the front page: "DOMESTIC TERRORISTS" SOUGHT IN AUDITORIUM ATTACK – BAND "JESSICA'S JONES" IMPLICATED IN VIOLENT UPRISING. There was a grainy photo of us on stage, mid-performance of "Patriot Games," my face contorted in a snarl, Jessica shredding her guitar, Leo's trumpet raised like a weapon. Below it, smaller, smudged photos of each of us, probably lifted from our university IDs. We were officially enemies of the state. Domestic terrorists. The words felt unreal, absurd, yet chillingly final. The sight sent a fresh wave of cold dread through me, colder than the desert night. There was no downplaying this, no hoping it would blow over. We were marked. Branded. Hunted.

The fragments of the song kept coming back to me then, a soundtrack to our flight, the only thing that felt remotely real in this surreal nightmare. *Remember singing 'bout being free? Felt so simple, you and me... Now freedom's just this patch of dark... This fading headlight, leaving marks... On empty roads... but you're still here... And that's the only thing that's clear...* I sketched the lines in my notebook later, back in the sweltering van, the melody taking shape, weary but tender, a fragile counterpoint to the harsh reality outside. Northbound Static. That's what it felt like. Moving through a world of noise and fear, searching for a clear signal, holding onto the fragile connections that remained, the shared breath in the darkness.

Days blurred into nights. We crossed a state line, then another, the signs changing – Welcome to Nevada, Welcome to Oregon – the landscape shifting, but the feeling of being hunted, of being adrift, remained a constant, unwelcome passenger. Leo's Canadian contacts were proving harder to reach than he'd anticipated, our lack of phones a major complication. He managed to use a public data terminal at a mega-truck stop – a risky move that had Mack pacing nervously outside – to send another coded message, but a reply would take time, and we couldn't stay put. We were burning through the little cash we had on gas and cheap food, sleeping cramped in the van or finding brief, uneasy refuge in hidden spots Mack scouted out.

Finally, after what felt like an eternity of tense, sleepless driving, Mack, still at the helm, her face drawn with exhaustion but her eyes alert, directed us off the main highway again, down a series of progressively smaller, rougher roads. We were somewhere deep in the Pacific Northwest, the air cooler now, smelling of pine and damp earth. The trees pressed in close, ancient giants forming a dense canopy overhead, blocking out the sky, swallowing the minivan in shadow.

"This is it for now," Mack said, pulling the van into a barely visible track leading to a dilapidated, abandoned-looking ranger station, half-hidden by overgrown bushes and ferns. Moss grew thick on the decaying wooden shingles. "We can lay low here for a day or two. Rest. Figure out the next move. Leo, try your contacts again when it's safe. We need a solid plan to cross the border."

The ranger station was little more than a shell, dusty and cobweb-strewn, smelling of mildew and rodent droppings, but it had four walls, and old-school USGS uplink wired up to a weather station, and a roof that didn't leak too badly. It felt like a small, temporary sanctuary, a place to finally stop running, if only for a moment. But the relief was muted by the gnawing uncertainty. We were still fugitives. Still a long way from Canada. Still a million miles from anything resembling safety or home.

As dusk settled, casting long, eerie shadows through the broken windowpanes, painting the dust motes dancing in the air gold, I sat on the creaking porch steps, my sketchbook in my lap, my bass leaning against the railing beside me like a weary companion. The melody for "Northbound Static" was almost complete in my head, a quiet hum against the backdrop of the whispering forest. Inside the dim station, I could hear the others settling down, the rustle of sleeping bags on the dusty floor, Leo's low murmur as he perhaps tried to reassure Jessica, Mack's quiet movements as she likely checked the perimeter again before taking her own rest.

We were broken, battered, and on the run. But we were still together. The air grew cool, the scent of pine sharp and clean. I watched the last sliver of sun disappear behind the towering trees, feeling the immense weight of everything we'd lost, everything we were running from, and the terrifying uncertainty of what lay ahead.

Just as a profound loneliness threatened to swallow me whole, I felt a presence beside me. Jessica sat down quietly on the step, close enough that our shoulders brushed. She didn't say anything, just looked out at the darkening forest with me. After a long moment, her hand found mine, her fingers hesitantly intertwining with mine. Her touch was cool, trembling slightly, but her grip was surprisingly firm. A silent acknowledgment. A shared breath in the vast, encroaching darkness. For now, maybe that was enough. Maybe that was the only signal clear enough to cut through the static.